MW01633930

Destiny of Daring

Never Forget

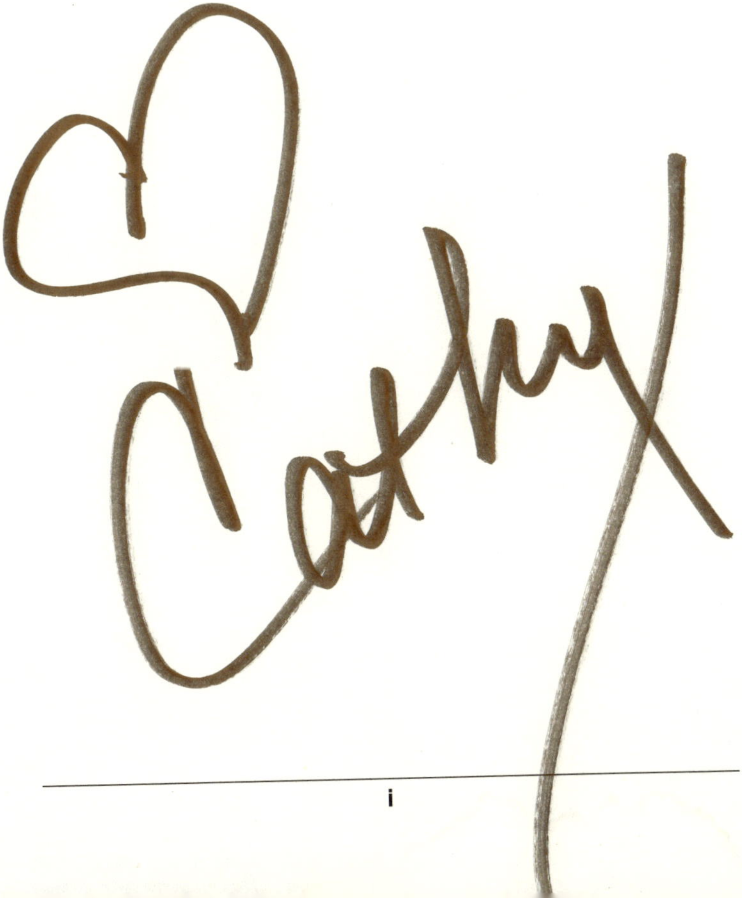

Destiny of
Daring

Never Forget

Cathy Burnham Martin

Quiet Thunder Publishing
Naples, FL   Manchester, NH   Columbus, NC

www.QTPublishing.com

This title and more are also featured at
www.GoodLiving123.com

Destiny of
Daring
Never Forget

Copyright © 2023 Quiet Thunder Publishing
Naples, FL   Manchester, NH   Columbus, NC

All rights reserved worldwide. No part of this book may be
reproduced in any form or by any means without prior
written permission from the publisher or authors, except for
the inclusion of brief quotations
embodied in critical essays, articles, or reviews,
or as permitted by law.
These articles and/or reviews must state
the correct title and author by name.

Paperback edition: ISBN 978-1-939220-68-4
eBook edition: ISBN 978-1-939220-69-1
Audiobook edition: ISBN 978-1-939220-70-7

Published and printed in the United States of America.
Library of Congress Control Number:
2023916512

Any references to historical events, real people, or real places are
used fictitiously. Other names, characters, places, and events are
products of the author's imagination. Any resemblance to actual
events, places, or people, living or dead, is entirely coincidental.

Dedication

I humbly dedicate this book to the millions of Armenians throughout the Diaspora. Whether you are Armenian by chance or Armenian by choice, the events leading to and following the official start of the Ottoman Empire's genocide against Armenians on April 24, 1915, remain part of our story forever.

These were times of tumultuous violence and great unknowns, as well as years of unimaginable human strength and loving mercy. Past events forever shape who we are today. For those of Armenian descent, the years of trouble in our ancestors' homelands open our hearts for pain but also remind us of the importance to always remember. For people with Turkish ancestry, acknowledging the violence perpetrated in the past is highly challenging and most unsavory but also delivers a calm peace and awareness that we humans can and must do better.

We are all one. If we try to erase, minimize, rationalize, or justify the horrific behaviors of our human race, we risk losing the essential lessons of history. Accepting our frailties and faux pas helps us to not repeat chapters we may prefer did not exist.

Throngs of Armenians rose from the ashes of despair, and these ancestors strove mightily to start again and build a better life for the next generations. They gave us a chance to live and to experience many freedoms they had never known, along with the challenge to forgive mightily. Each day we have a powerful responsibility to our forefathers and mothers to live better, to not lose faith, and to never forget.

Cathy Burnham Martin

Table of Contents

Back Matter

Foreword

Ah, Armenia. My deepest family roots hail from the ancient kingdom of Van, which stood as a chief center of the Urartu kingdom and what became known as Anatolia from the 1200s to the 800s BC. Armenia and Armenians then became part of the Median, the Macedonian, and the Roman/Byzantine Empires. Armenia then became the first to adopt Christianity as its national religion in 301 AD. In the 1500s, Armenia became part of the Ottoman Empire as it swept into the Middle East, Europe and North Africa.

Sadly, after varying periods with limited autonomy, Armenians were dealt with harshly, to say the very least. In the waning decades of the Ottoman Empire, Christians became openly blamed by the government for Ottoman failures, including territorial losses throughout Europe and North Africa. As Muslim refugees fled from those lost areas, lands we now know as Turkey faced increasing population, poverty, disease, and famine.

The Young Turks leadership took full advantage of the coming Great War. Periodic waves of massacres escalated the standard social and financial anti-Christian discrimination. Finally, under the guise of preparation for war and assisting returning Muslim refugees, an official plan was devised and launched to deport Armenians to the Syrian desert. In truth, this was a thinly veiled program to eliminate Christians.

Book 3 in the Destiny trilogy unravels family experiences in the Ottoman Empire. The times were difficult, and the cultures may feel distant.

While I understand that Armenian names can seem tricky, I let them stand. For example, Aghavni is pronounced

AUV-nee. Hrant sounds like her-AUNT, with the British pronunciation of aunt. Emine sounds like EEE-min, and Halime sounds like HAHL-ih may. Nane sounds like NAH-nay. Last names ending in -ian or -yan can also appear daunting. For example, Gulumian sounds like Goo-LOO-mee-an. This book takes the Gulumian story to Constantinople (Istanbul) from its historic home at the base of Mount Ararat in the city of Van, which is pronounced like the number "one" with a "v" in front of it. Let all the names and historical places help absorb you into the ancient culture.

The Destiny trilogy tells true stories, not just a saga based on a true story. In launching the trilogy, I needed very little creative freedom with my own grandfather's remembrances. And I am honored to now also intertwine a few stories that reflect the experiences of family friends.

This final book in the trilogy delivers answers to some questions and leaves others for future generations to unravel. During this adventure, we look at some modern-day perspective and reflect on actual historic events in the old country from 1915 and the years that immediately followed.

With the deepest respect, I bring you both the loving family times and those revealing the inhumane violence perpetrated by a failing government. Calling these "difficult times" may be the largest understatement of all.

Some images can be hauntingly horrific, but I include no gratuitous violence. There is simply no way to sugarcoat the arduous experiences of people struggling through times of our most hideous exercises in man's inhumanity against man.

Cathy Burnham Martin

Some Characters from Books 1 and 2 in the Destiny Trilogy

Here are some characters from the Destiny trilogy's Books 1 and 2 referenced in Book 3. Readers will also meet some new characters. (Some real names have been altered.)

Garabed Ohanes Gulumian – 1870-1915 Van, Armenia; tradesman, and tailor; ambushed and executed by Ottoman Turks in late April 1915.

Aghavni Gadara (Samargian) Gulumian – born 1871 in Salmast, Armenia; married Garabed Gulumian in 1887; immigrated to US 08/06/1916 with youngest sons Vahram and Hrant. Died in Salisbury, NH in 1956.

Their children:

Ohannes Garabed Gulumian – born 11/08/1888 in Van, Armenia; immigrated to US in 1909; died in Salisbury, NH in 1963 at age 75.

Aram Garabed Gulumian – born 11/28/1893 in Van, Armenia; immigrated to US 6/30/1912; died in Salisbury, NH in 1972 at age 79.

Vahram Garabed Gulumian – born 3/26/1898 in Van, Armenia; died in Boston, MA in 1926 at age 27 of pernicious anemia, a rare blood disorder.

Nazeli Gulumian – born 3/26/1898; Vahram's twin sister; engaged to marry Toros Kherbekian; raped and shot by Ottoman Turks in Gulumian home 1915.

Anush Gulumian – born 5/1/1901; youngest daughter of Garabed and Aghavni; raped and shot by Ottoman Turks in Gulumian home in 1915.

Hrant Garabed Gulumian – born 3/6/1906 in Van, Armenia; youngest son of Garabed and Aghavni; 9 years old when he, brother Vahram, and mother Aghavni escaped marauding Ottoman Turkish soldiers in 1915; died at age 63 in Goffstown, NH in 1969.

Marjorie Rowe Gulumian – born 3/22/1908 in New Hampshire. Married Hrant Gulumian. Disowned by her family for marrying a foreigner. Mother of Hrant's three daughters. Died in NH in 2001 at the age of 93.

Great-Grandchild:

Cassie – Hrant Gulumian's 2nd granddaughter; became author and chronicled the Gulumian stories.

Gulumian Family Friends:

Serkan Raffi – elder Turkish officer who witnessed the ambush and executions of Aghavni Gulumian's husband and father; Serkan's wife was Halime.

Aydin Raffi – son of Serkan and Halime Raffi; childhood friend of Aram Gulumian

Hulianna Terlemezian – Aghavni Gulumian's best friend; emigrated to the United States and moved to New Hampshire with her son's family. Sister-in-law of Garabed's friend Grigor Terlemezian.

Dajad Terlemezian – born circa 1890; son of Hulianna; celebrated Armenian hero who assassinated the Armenian traitor Davajan Davo in March 1908. Moved his family to Salisbury, New Hampshire to join the Gulumians.

Toros Kherbekian – 2nd son of Garabed Gulumian's merchant friend Kherbekian; engaged Nazeli Gulumian; forced into Turkish military service; Turks disarmed and shot his entire unit. Unknown to Aghavni and her children, Toros and one other Armenian survived.

Arriving Now

1

THE TIRES OF the giant Boeing 787 scuffed the tarmac at London's Heathrow Airport. Cassie had not slept a wink in the 7 hours since departing from New York's JFK Airport.

Her mind raced. More than one hundred years had passed since Ottoman soldiers invaded her grandfather's home in Van, Armenia, injuring his mother, while raping and shooting Hrant's two older sisters. At 9 years old, he and his older, but sickly brother, had been disguised as little girls in hopes they would be spared the slaughter that had been raining down on young Armenian boys.

The Gulumian family had been about to flee. They were merely awaiting the anticipated return home of Hrant's father and grandfather. Sadly, that never happened as their small party of merchants was ambushed, and the two men were murdered by the soldiers just outside their city gates.

Cassie had learned the sordid saga from her grandfather Hrant back when she was barely a teenager. She had been horrified to learn of the soldiers' dishonoring attacks on both of his sisters, followed by their shootings. Cassie had marveled at his mother's fortitude and struggle to help her two remaining children survive, escape, and seek safety in Kars, Russia. Cassie had wept with both heartache and joy as she learned Hrant's life story of coming to America, the challenges of being a foreigner, his pride in becoming a US citizen, and the fulfillment of raising a family.

She had also treasured the one and only item that had survived her family's emigration process. Her Great Grandmother Aghavni had managed to hide her most precious possession all the way to America... her gold wedding ring, which was three rings delicately hinged together at the base, and featuring two clasped hands, each on its own band. When opened, they revealed a third band with two entwined hearts in the center.

When Hrant grew up and married Marjorie in 1930, Aghavni had given her treasured ring to her youngest son. Marjorie wore it for a time on a long golden chain, but feared she might damage the only family heirloom.

She and Hrant had then given it to Cassie when she was a teenager in the 1960s. They had been helping her through some dark, emotional struggles caused by a severe recurring nightmare. When Cassie finally shared the dreams horrific details, her grandfather had shocked them all.

Though he had never spoken of their turmoil in Armenia since coming to America, the verbal floodgates had suddenly opened. Though he could not explain how, Cassie had just described his family and home back in Van, Armenia. The lass somehow knew every detail. Jaws dropped when he proclaimed that if there was such a thing as reincarnation, he knew that Cassie had been his sister, Anush. Many more afternoons of story sharing followed. The Armenian connection was indeed a powerful one between Hrant and his granddaughter Cassie. His mother's wedding ring immediately became her most treasured possession.

Cassie had long pondered what could and should be done to preserve the ring and the story behind it. She had become a stepmother of four, but she had not borne children. Then she thought about a niece and her nephews. She considered a cousin's son and daughter. The time was coming when action needed to be taken. Approaching 70 years of age, Cassie was an older woman herself now. Steps needed to be taken to preserve history and the multitude of similar family stories embodied in her Great Grandmother Aghavni Gulumian's precious wedding ring.

In 2014, she successfully published Marjorie Gulumian's memoirs. "Of the Same Blood: Your Eurasian Heritage," which included Hrant's harrowing story of escape from the Ottoman Turks. She knew that was not enough, as the ring still needed more than just the pages of a nonfiction journal.

Several times, she had started to write her grandfather's story as a novel. The tale was hauntingly dark and difficult to write. She put the papers away more than once before finally choosing to share the details as historical fiction.

Recalling some words of her grandfather gave her strength. He often had recalled various Armenian proverbs that his own father had frequently shared. On this occasion, she remembered, 'Begin with small things, that you may achieve great.'

"Ah, yes," she thought. "One step at a time."

Then came the mysterious phone call from London. The voice of an elderly woman she had never met was claiming to be the daughter of Nazeli, one of Hrant Gulumian's sisters thought to have died in the soldiers' invasion of their home in Armenia. Miraculous was the only word that came to mind. Though it all seemed impossible, it was true... One of her grandfather's sisters had survived the Ottoman soldiers' attack back in 1915 in Van, Armenia.

How could Cassie possibly have slept on this flight? She was about to meet a centenarian... Sidika, the daughter of Grampa Hrant's sister... a woman that no one knew had even lived through the evil events of the Ottoman genocide of Armenians.

Had Cassie not published her grandmother's memoirs, Sidika would not have known what had happened to her own grandmother and uncles either. Sidika's daughter Nuray had periodically searched the Internet. The Gulumian name had been one of those she regularly sought. Then she found the memoir. Both she and her mother read it with great interest.

Nuray and Sidika recognized a long-lost connection to their Armenian roots. They learned Cassie's contact information and reached out immediately. Now the ladies were about to meet. Cassie's heart pounded with anticipation. She strode with a hurried pace toward the airport's secured area exit.

New Beginnings

2

A SIGN BEARING her name caught Cassie's eyes. A middle-aged woman held the sign, and Cassie immediately knew the elderly woman sitting in a wheelchair beside her must be Nazeli's daughter. She smiled and rushed toward the two women, tears spontaneously rushing down her cheeks.

"I am Cassie! I am Cassie!"

She gushed, dropped her carry-on bag, and bubbled out their names, too. Nuray dropped the sign she had been holding and wrapped her arms around Cassie. Both women found themselves spontaneously laughing and crying at the same time.

Cassie then dropped to her knees, coming face to face with the elder woman. She looked very frail, but the smile on Sidika's face was crystal clear. Tears flowed from all three women's eyes, and Sidika extended both her arms. Her hands motioned Cassie to come to her.

As they embraced, Cassie began to sob. Her stomach muscles heaved with unbridled emotion. Oh, how deeply Grampa Hrant would have cherished this moment! One of his dear sisters had not only lived, but she had family alive and well in England.

Regaining their composure, the three women shared formal greetings. After gathering Cassie's suitcase at the baggage reclaim area, they headed for the Heathrow

Express train to London. Cassie couldn't help but marvel at the modern train system, with arrivals and departures every fifteen minutes.

"We Americans have so much we should learn about mass transportation," Cassie stated simply. "The train systems in Europe always impress me."

"I must apologize," interjected Nuray. "Often, I believe we have too many choices. In this case, I believe we are best to simply take the Tube."

She observed the confused look on Cassie's face. Nuray smiled and continued. "The Piccadilly or purple line of our London Underground is a local. However, even with more than a dozen stops, we still can hop on right here at Heathrow's underground station and make no changes until we reach our destination at Knightsbridge Station."

Her mother had not commented until this point. "My darling, Nuray. Might it not be faster to travel on the Express?"

"Oh, Mama," continued Nuray. "I mean no disrespect. The Heathrow Express will make the journey into London in less than 20 minutes. However, we would then have to change platforms at Paddington Station for Bakerloo and then change platforms again for the westbound Piccadilly, and then still would have to go 3 stops to get to Knightsbridge. Express *sounds* faster, but when all is said and done, I believe it will take substantially longer. Worse yet, ups and downs and changing platforms would not be good for you. If you want to take the Express, we can do that, but I will insist on hiring a hackney when we get to Paddington."

Sidika smiled at Nuray. She gently reached out and patted her hand before she spoke. "You are completely correct, my dear. I was merely testing you. My mother used to say, 'He who speaks a lot, learns little.' But you also listen very well."

Sighing, Nuray turned to Cassie as they moved down the platform to board the Piccadilly line train. "Mama insists on me maintaining my independent thinking and my ability to speak about what's on my mind."

"I learned that from my own Mama," said Cassie. "And the proverb Sidika just shared reminds me so much of my Grandpa Hrant!"

"Oh, yes. Mama learned many Armenian proverbs from her mother. And, though it flew in the face of social norms, my Grandmother Emine was fiercely protective of the rare freedoms she knew to both study books and languages and also to speak her mind back in old Armenia and ever since."

After getting Sidika comfortably seated, Cassie posed her question to the elder woman. "Emine? I am confused. I thought your mother's name was Nazeli? That was the name of my Grampa Hrant's older sister."

"Ah, yes. I understand. For her protection during the deportation marches, her given Armenian name Nazeli was changed to the Turkish name Emine."

As the train rolled and stopped at its various stations, Sidika explained further. "I have it all written down. Mama did not want anything to become lost or forgotten. She and Papa both wrote several letters to my now dearly departed brother and me. Her story is best in her own Armenian words. We will get you checked into the Beaufort Hotel. Then, if you are not too tired from your travels, we will go to our flat. Though we are thoroughly British Turks, Nuray has been a good student of both Armenian and Turkish languages. She will read my mother's story to you."

The conversation then switched to focus on Sidika and Nuray's questions about Cassie and life in America. Cassie found her thoughts split dreadfully. She wanted to be respectful and answer all their questions, but her mind remained heavily focused on what she might be about to learn. Finally, they reached the Knightsbridge station.

Cassie had booked a room at the Beaufort in Knightsbridge because The Cadogan Hotel had been purchased and closed for extensive renovations. She had enjoyed staying at The Cadogan with her husband a few years earlier, and she was sorry to not be able to go back there. She found all its history and literary guests fascinating. From America's Mark Twain to Irish poet Oscar Wilde, she could easily picture the boutique hotel's gala life in its heyday.

She thought it fitting that The Cadogan Hotel was now getting a massive, multi-million-dollar rehab. She could stay there on her next visit. For now, Cassie simply glowed as her anticipation billowed.

Knightsbridge
3

CASSIE REALIZED THAT the Knightsbridge section of London was home to a very lavish residential neighborhood, and some of the city's finest boutique hotels, restaurants, and shopping. Its population was vibrantly large and diverse.

She had expected to hear many different languages. Cassie smiled as she pondered her own ignorance and surprise upon hearing the proper British English being spoken all around her as they strolled through the neighborhood.

Sidika's flat was luxuriously expansive. Warm, late morning sunlight streamed through the large windows, reflecting off the polished hardwood floors. Highly detailed, hand-woven rugs sat neatly placed under the heavy, upholstered furniture. Crocheted lace doilies on side tables protected additional doilies. Her possessions were expensive, valued, and, obviously, well taken care of by Sidika.

The elder woman lowered herself rather gracefully onto an intricately embroidered chaise, reclining a bit to relax. She gestured for Cassie to sit on a lush velvet sofa beside her. As she did so, Nuray sat across from her and opened a large binder of papers. Most appeared hand-written. Some were more recently typed.

As Nuray sorted through the pages with great care, she placed them in several little piles, as if lining up her grandmother's story in chronological order. These pages obviously contained precious family information.

The last details that Cassie had known about Nazeli included the fact that she was engaged to marry a dear childhood friend, Toros Kherbekian, the son of a merchant friend of her family. He had been forced to join the Ottoman army, and they were set to be married when he returned. However, his entire Armenian regiment was marched into a field, disarmed, shot, and left for dead. Although unknown by the Gulumians at the time, only Toros and one other young Armenian man managed to survive their injuries.

As the remaining Gulumians were being helped to escape from Van, Armenia, Hrant and his mother Aghavni had miraculously found Toros in the caves that were being used to hide weapons, Armenian Ottoman Army deserters, and injured Armenians. They had given Toros the sad news that Nazeli and her sister Anush had been shot by the Ottoman soldiers.

But now it turns out that Nazeli had somehow survived! Did Toros and Nazeli find each other again?

Nuray began, "My grandmother, the woman you know as Nazeli, led an amazing life. It was not the life she had thought was her future, but she worked hard to turn dark, personal disasters into a truly golden destiny.

"Personally, I cannot imagine seeing or enduring even a percentage of what she did. I remind myself that many had an even tougher life than she did, though some had one with far greater ease. She made the problematic decision to hide in plain sight, one might say."

"I don't understand." That was all Cassie could say.

Now Sidika spoke. "Please know, Miss Cassie, that my mother never knew that her twin brother, baby brother Hrant, and mother successfully escaped. She hoped, but she never knew. Finally, she had to accept that they had fallen victim to massacre, or disease, or starvation on one of the many deportation marches toward the Syrian deserts. The few Armenians who made it to the camps alive, suffered greatly, as the Ottomans often withheld food and water from the Armenians in what became death camps.

"Mother felt fortunate to have been rescued by Turkish family friends, but that also meant having to pretend to be Muslim to survive. Had their ruse failed, that Turkish family would have also been put to death for sympathizing with, never mind befriending or helping an Armenian. The Ottomans were not particularly open-minded about such things."

"Oh, my goodness." Cassie sat quietly, just shaking her head. "Please. Tell me what you can."

Sidika nodded. "Initially, my mother stayed very quiet about her Armenian background. Even when the new Turkish Republic was formed, leaders fanned the flames of hatred for Armenians. In many areas, distrust and hatred grew. We children... my older brother and I... grew up not knowing our mother was Armenian. This was the norm for all children born of mixed parentage. This means that *we* are Armenians, though we thought we were only Turkish.

"I was nearly an adult before Mama and Papa shared their story. We were shocked. And yet, we also felt great pride regarding the actions of those on both sides of our family. Both Turkish and Armenian relatives exhibited great courage and bravery.

"As time went on, we eventually also learned that the vast majority of the Ottoman Sultans also did not have full Turkish blood. The mothers of 35 of the 36 Sultans were not Turkish at all. Most were Armenian, or else Russian, Jewish, or Greek. We began to realize that my brother and I were in very good company, as the Ottomans had intermixed with western Christians and others for many generations, several centuries, in fact.

Armenian, Greek, and Jewish women were being educated. It turns out that the sultans found their intelligence and beauty more attractive than women who had no education."

Sidika now looked toward Nuray, who picked up her first bundle of pages. She then began.

Nazeli Awakens

4

WAILING WOMEN'S VOICES and crying children. A sharp pain in her left shoulder. The aroma of hot chicken soup.

Nazeli inhaled again. Everything felt fuzzy and foggy in a most peculiar way.

Suddenly, she shuddered with awareness and attempted to sit up. Pain coursed through her left side. Nazeli softly cried out as her body slumped back.

At this moment, she felt panic... again. She was waking up in a strange place... a sparse bedroom she had never seen. She felt weak and frightened. Never had she felt such pain as she was now experiencing in her chest. The intensity made it nearly impossible to breathe. As she slowly regained consciousness, her memory became clear.

She did not dare move. She opened her eyes slowly. Without turning her head, she glanced about the room. She recognized nothing. She closed her eyes and tried to think.

The last thing she could remember was total chaos. Oh, yes. Ottoman soldiers storming into their home and dragging her into the courtyard suddenly freshened her mind. Both she and her younger sister Anush were cursed at and ravaged repeatedly by three different soldiers.

She remembered hearing her mother calling out to them. Aghavni pleaded repeatedly for her daughters to survive the assault by these beasts.

Her highly spirited younger sister Anush had struggled wildly but to no avail. Nazeli recalled thinking that her sister should not have kept fighting back. And she remembered feeling utterly numb as one of the soldiers brutalizing Anush pulled out his pistol and shot her dead, splattering Nazeli with her sister's blood.

Now, knowing her own fate, Nazeli had uttered silent prayers. Her eyelids had been closed when she felt her third attacker rise and spit on her face, before the second shot rang out. Everything then went blank.

Unable to squelch the painful memories, Nazeli now heard approaching footsteps. She closed her eyes.

The next thing she felt was a warm, moist cloth gently wiping her brow. In Turkish, she heard a familiar woman's voice.

"You, poor dear. This should never have happened to you. To any of you."

Oh, my. She was hearing Halime Raffi, a close friend of her family. She opened her eyes.

"Oh, Nazeli," Halime began. "Do not try to move. You have been shot, but you are safe now, my dear."

Nazeli's language skills paid off instantly. Her Turkish was very good.

"How did I get here," Nazeli asked the kindly woman. Such details were more than a nonexistent blur to her.

"My husband found you. He had promised your mother that he would take your body and your sister's body to your priest. But later he discovered that you were still breathing, so, with the help of his nephew, he hid you here in our home."

Halime now proceeded to change the bandage over Nazeli's wound. Fortunately, the shot that was meant to kill her had missed her heart and her lungs. Her shoulder would heal.

Just then, Serkan Raffi returned home. Upon hearing the women's voices, he entered the room.

"Ah," he began. "You have finally awakened."

"How long have I been here?" Nazeli had no sense of the time that had passed.

"We brought you here 3 days ago," Serkan answered. "You have not regained consciousness until just now."

"Mother! Little Hrant! My twin brother Vahram! Ohhhh, he was so frail and sickly. Are they alright?"

Serkan tilted his head, indicating that he did not know. "They were forced into a deportation group with a destination in the Syrian Desert, but I had already heard that this group would not be taken more than one mile outside the city. So, I secretly told your mother of the urgency to escape from that group while still in the walled city of Van."

"And did she? Did my mother and brothers escape?"

"In total honesty, I do not know."

Nazeli gasped, as Serkan immediately continued.

"There is a report of a small group running away. However, I have not received confirmation as to whether or not this was your family. I can tell you that I was able to find the actual place where the Armenians were..."

Serkan paused. "How should I say this? Perhaps it is best if I simply say that I inspected the bodies and did not recognize anyone from your family. My superior officer questioned me to learn why I was checking all the bodies, and I had to tell him that I was trying to be certain that no one had been left alive."

"This is disgusting! Inhumane!" Nazeli was aghast. "Why do some of your people hate us so deeply? What have we ever done to them?"

"Please, my dear." Serkan's wife now spoke up. "You must rest."

Serkan added, "You have done nothing except be Christian in a world they believe should all be Muslim. And now they use the cover of this Great War as an opportunity to answer what they have called 'the Armenian question.' They are clearing all Armenians out of Turkey, primarily from your six major provinces."

"So, killing us is their solution? Taxing us and treating us as second-class citizens was not enough?""

"Nazeli, Halime is correct. You must rest." Serkan continued. "I will keep seeking information on your family's whereabouts."

"Toros. Could you locate my fiancé, Toros Kherbekian?" Nazeli added, "He was conscripted into an Armenian contingent in the Ottoman Army, and we have not heard from him now in several months."

"I will do my best." Serkan Raffi nodded. In truth, he held little hope that he would get the good news she obviously sought.

Though Muslim, his family and the Gulumians had been dear friends for years, albeit secretly. Clandestine meetings were the only way that Christians and Muslims could associate as friends in the increasingly formidable political environment surrounding the waning Ottoman Empire.

It also seemed that the more territories the Empire lost, the angrier the Young Turks became. As the Ottomans lost lands in Eastern Europe and northern Africa, their frustrations were increasingly aimed at the Armenians. As Muslim refugees arrived from those areas, the Young Turks had started taking lands and homes from the Christians, both Armenians and Greeks, to supply their Muslim citizens.

"For now," Serkan continued. "Please focus your energy on healing. Our time here grows short, and we must help you to be able to travel."

Hard Facts
5

NAZELI HEALED. SERKAN Raffi and his wife kept her safe. They treated her as a daughter. Still, her recovery process was a slow one.

Their nephew Yavuz had never been close to Nazeli's family, but he respected his aunt and uncle. He knew they had carried on a forbidden friendship with the Christian Armenian family.

Now Yavuz regularly brought food, clean water, and other supplies to the Raffi home. And he checked in on her each time.

However, sleep, never mind peaceful sleep, remained elusive. Gunfire hailed almost continuously. Ottoman cannons pounded the Armenian quarters in waves. The once lovely Gulumian home was among those that had been demolished. The ceaseless cries of widows and orphaned children haunted everyone's thoughts.

Both Serkan and Halime apologized, repeatedly, for all the harm the Ottomans had done to Nazeli's family... and to so many other Armenian families.

"You must not blame yourselves," insisted Nazeli. "These vicious acts have not been perpetrated by you. Quite the opposite. You rescued me at great personal risk. If your leaders learn that you have been protecting me, the punishment will be harsh."

"Nazeli, please know that we find the attacks on and deaths of your father, your grandfather, and your younger sister to be unconscionable." Now Serkan lowered his face before continuing. "But the pain for you does not stop there. I hardly know how to begin to tell you my latest information."

The teen shook her head as she spoke. "I do not know how my weary heart could possibly be wounded any more deeply than it already has been. Please. Tell me what you have learned. Please."

As an elder, but low-ranking Ottoman officer, Serkan Raffi was not being included in the ongoing attacks against the Armenians. His orders had come to transfer to Constantinople as part of a training team. However, he also remained privy to a great deal of information.

"My dear, do you remember how I explained to you what happened after you and your sister were shot?"

Nazeli nodded her head. Halime sat on the edge of the bed and held Nazeli's hand as her husband continued.

"When the soldiers pulled your mother and younger brothers into that first deportation group to leave Van, please remember that I had desperately pleaded with them to flea before the group reached the South Gate. At any cost! I was sure that Aghavni understood the urgency of escaping and hiding *before* the group was led out of the walled city. I have continued checking with my sources, and it has now been confirmed that the trio did run away."

"Then this is good news! Very good news. Why do you look sad?"

Serkan calmly continued. "The soldiers had initially failed to find them, although they insisted that they searched many streets. The bad news is that other soldiers now report finding them on the road. They were running away."

"No, no, no!" Alarm rang in Nazeli's voice. "That is not possible! We were going to run away, but our plans were to completely *avoid* the roads! Papa had given us strict instructions not to travel on the roads. This must be a lie!"

Halime now wrapped her arm around the trembling girl. "I am terribly sorry, Nazeli."

Serkan spoke very softly now. "The soldiers have assured our superiors that the Gulumian family would not get the opportunity to escape again. Nazeli, I am sorry. But they are gone."

Nazeli's head dropped as she began to weep. Her grief had no end.

"I wish that was the end of my sad news," Serkan added. "Unfortunately, I have also tracked down the Armenian work contingent in the neighboring province... the one to which your fiancé, Toros was assigned."

"Nooooo," Nazeli moaned. "You cannot possibly be about to tell me that they have taken everything and everyone from me."

"Though it is dreadful, I know. His entire unit is gone."

Serkan felt no need to fill the stricken young woman in on the gory details. Nazeli's fiancé, Toros Kherbekian, had been shot in cold blood, along with all his fellow Armenian soldiers while lined up in a field in the province of Bitlis, across Lake Van.

Then, of course, the Ottoman Army had been shelling all the Armenian quarters of Van, both those within and outside the walls. Guards had been posted around the Raffi home to keep them safe from any potential retaliation attacks by angry Armenians. This would give them time to prepare for departure.

However, now they must flee. Reports confirmed that the Russian troops were advancing quickly. They were coming to help the Armenians. Within hours, the family would need to join the refugees trying to flee from the area.

Confessions

6

CHRISTIAN AND MUSLIM refugees alike were running for their lives. Many Muslim refugees were newly locating in areas that would become known as Turkey. They lacked community roots and a depth of neighbors and friends.

Christians ran to try and escape massacre or deportation. Ottoman troops were slaughtering Armenians, and retaliation attacks were now reported. Thus, Muslims also ran to stay out of the way of understandably impassioned Armenians.

To complicate matters more, the Ottoman troops were now killing Muslim families. Many Muslims were discovered to be harboring their Christian friends. The Young Turks' leaders became furious at the increasing reports of this, as they had made it very clear that fraternizing with the Armenians would not be tolerated.

And yet, they felt a powerful need to prevent the outside world from learning that they were killing their own Christian and Muslim civilian populations. Serkan's nephew Yavuz arrived with the latest report.

"Uncle, the governor just read the new orders. Prime Minister Talaat Pasha has ordered us to openly blame the Armenians every time our troops kill Muslim civilians for sympathizing with Christians. Further, they now want us to go door-to-door to inspect and find Muslim homes that are harboring our enemies. If

Armenians are found, then we are to deem them and the Turks as traitors. All such enemies are to then be... eliminated."

"Oh, Yavuz, this bad news is not unexpected." Serkan continued. "I have heard talk of this action previously. Plus, I have received reports of this same response already being carried out in other provinces."

The two men looked at Halime and Nazeli. They then looked at each other and nodded.

"Nazeli," began Serkan. "The time has come to disguise you. Those of us here in this room are the only ones who know that you are here, and we must now make you one of us. This does not mean that we will force you to become a Muslim, although that is an approved means of saving your life."

"What can I do?" Nazeli implored sincerely.

"Your Turkish speaking skills are excellent, so we must now all pretend that you are Turkish, and not Armenian." Serkan looked into her eyes. "Can you do this?"

"Yes, I believe I can. You have all been so kind to me. But the last thing I want to do is cause you trouble or put any of you in further danger. I think I am well enough to travel now, but I also think that I should travel alone. You have all risked enough."

Serkan shook his head. "No. There is much you do not yet know, so you cannot possibly understand. I made a vow to help your family in any way I can. To this point, however, I have failed greatly."

"Oh, no," Nazeli objected. "You are not responsible for my family's heartaches and losses. You saved my life after the Turkish soldiers had left me for dead. If my father was alive now, he would say that *we* owe *you* everything."

"Ahhhh, your father." Serkan sighed. He then reached out, taking both of Nazeli's hands in his own before he continued. "Garabed Gulumian, your father, was a dear friend of mine. Though I had not known in advance who was to be the target on that dreadful early morning, I..."

Now Serkan openly wept, and his voice cracked deeply as he spoke. "I was among the troops there on that hateful day. While I was powerless to stop it, I ended up being a witness to the ambush and executions of your father and grandfather. I saw the officer in charge shoot two of your father's traveling companions for protesting.

"I felt complete shame for staying silent, and I felt the deepest respect as I observed their extreme bravery and stoic calm. Your father and grandfather thanked each other. Your grandfather specifically thanked your father with words I will never forget. He thanked him for always having 'shown courage, honor, and strong character.'

"Your father quietly prayed to God to love and protect his family. As I listened to them, I felt blessed to have known them and yet regretful that I had taken their friendship for granted. And yes, I felt utterly ashamed that I lacked the courage to step forward and try to stop their executions. I heard the officer in charge hissing that 'Armenians were heathens and a blight on the earth that must be eliminated.' I am Turkish, but I was embarrassed to be associated with such ignorance, intolerance, and hatred."

A few moments of silence passed. Serkan's eyelids were closed, and yet his tears still flowed down his cheeks.

Nazeli felt numb. Here it was, yet another wound to her heart. Was she out of tears, or was her heart simply hardening?

This Turkish man she had always seen as so confident and strong now looked weak and somehow small sitting before her. Nazeli studied the vulnerability on Serkan's face before she spoke.

The Plan
7

"YOU HAVE LET unnecessary guilt and grief swallow you whole," Nazeli began. "You must learn to forgive yourself. You did not cause any of this. If you had tried to intervene on that fateful morning, you surely would have been killed. Then your family would also have lost its father. That would only have triggered more loss."

Serkan now looked up at the young woman. He could not imagine how she could even think about forgiveness amidst the hailstorm of grief that pummeled her. Nazeli softly continued.

"I will always remember and cherish my father for sharing sage remarks. Papa valued his ancestors' teachings. He often taught us by using old proverbs. If he were with us now, he would likely say something like, 'Far from the eye, far from the heart.' Perhaps it is good that you witnessed that ambush and their executions. Now the Young Turks will never be able to sell you their lies, because the truth has been seen by you first-hand. The truth now lives in your heart, as it lives in ours."

The elder man pondered his response, shaking his head slowly. "Sadly, had I not personally known your father, I might not have recognized the truth. I might have believed the lies being screamed at the men, just as I am sure most of the other Turkish soldiers likely did. But you are right. Because my eyes have seen all they have, the truth will always live in my heart.

"Further, you should know that on that day I vowed to learn exactly why Garabed and his father were targeted for that deadly ambush. Sadly, I learned it was because of words from one of your own clergy. My superior officers proudly announced that one of the lesser members of your church had been informing on his fellow Armenians."

Serkan scoffed loudly now. "This man thought these acts of sedition would somehow save his own skin. In truth, it got him sent to prison as soon as the siege on Van began. The guards there tortured him, trying to gain detailed information on the Armenian resistance. All they learned was that he had given them names of innocent families, like the Gulumians. The man knew nothing. His final confession got him tortured to death."

Nazeli sat very still. She now spoke not a word. But she thought of plenty of words, the kindest of which hailed from an old Armenian proverb. "Priest on the outside; Satan on the inside." Lies told by a trusted Christian leader had caused several deaths, including in her own family.

She recalled learning that many years earlier an Armenian traitor had revealed a secret stockpile of weapons and ammunition that Armenians had been gradually gathering and hiding in a nearby monastery. He had been hunted down and eliminated by a young man now touted as an Armenian hero. Dajad Terlemezian was the son of Hulianna, her mother's closest friend. Nazeli felt proud that he was a friend of her family.

No time remained to ponder the behavior and questionable choices people continued to make. The limited zone where the Raffi home sat now in relative safety would soon be overrun by Russian military troops.

Nazeli saw no reason to not travel with the Raffi family. None of her friends likely remained here in her city. If any had stayed, they were probably in hiding. Despite Serkan's efforts to locate specific people, it seemed that all the Gulumians' Armenian friends and neighbors had either fled or been marched away in the forced deportations. Of course, Nazeli was not about to share the information she knew about the Armenian resistance or the underground gathering and hiding places. She could only hope that some friends were safely holed up there.

Halime now returned the group's focus to the issues at hand. "Nazeli, the Turkish soldiers who will be escorting us to the harbor know that we do not have a daughter your age. A female may not travel, even in these dastardly times, without a male relative to accompany her. Please consider our plan, as we all must depart today." She glanced at Serkan, who nodded.

Serkan continued explaining the details. "Yavuz will travel with us, and we will all pretend... in name only... that you are his wife."

Nazeli's eyebrows rose, and she glanced at Yavuz. He nodded. Serkan then added, "He is not known here, so it will not be surprising that his wife is not known either. We must also stop calling you Nazeli because it is an Armenian name. As the head of this household, it is my obligation to name all children. By default, the duty to name you falls to me. Having prayed on this, Emine is the Turkish name I have selected for you. While it may be an unfamiliar name to you, I believe it is highly appropriate, as it means 'one who is fearless and courageous.' You most certainly live up to that meaning."

Halime spoke again. "As the women in our family, you and I will stay close together as we travel. We will keep our heads covered and our faces tilted down, so it is unlikely that someone will recognize you. Plus, you and I will be able to speak together a bit, although very quietly. You must only speak Turkish, as you primarily do with us. Please also try to remember that in our culture, women do not speak up unless invited to do so, and especially not in public."

Halime, Serkan, and Yavus all looked at Nazeli, awaiting her agreement. She looked in everyone's eyes before speaking. She nodded as she started to speak.

"I will be forever grateful for the kindness and courage you have all shown me. And it will be my honor to travel with you as we leave this place. The once lavish, ancient walled city of Van holds nothing but memories for me. I will pray for the strength to let the good memories of the past overtake the painful memories of the present. Nazeli will... remain here. As Emine, I will gratefully now step forward with you all."

She continued. "First, to the man who now becomes my uncle... my amca. Amca Serkan, thank you for saving my life and for proving to be as great a friend as a friend can be.

"And I thank you, Yavus. You do not know me well, so I appreciate that taking this great risk was not likely your idea."

Lastly, Nazeli, now Emine turned to Halime. "And because you are my aunt, my hala, I also thank you Hala Halime. My clothes were torn and greatly soiled, but you have repaired them. And you preserved my petticoat along with the one my poor sister Anush had been wearing. As you now know, our mother had stitched many secret pockets in which she had hidden coins and jewelry to aid in our planned escape... should we have become separated. We have been separated indeed. So, though we must leave behind larger items, several of which you were protecting for my family, please know that what little treasure I have will now be used to help us all travel to find safety."

Halime wrapped both her arms around her new "niece." After they hugged, Halime lifted her scarf from her shoulders and skillfully wrapped it around her head and neck. Emine followed suit. Halime nodded her approval, tucking in a long lock of Emine's hair. Without any further words, Serkan and Yavus led the group out the door.

Escape
8

NAZELI, NOW EMINE, felt extremely uncomfortable walking through the streets with Turkish soldiers escorting them. She kept her eyes cast downward as much as possible, as if someone might recognize her or discover that she was an Armenian.

She could not help but wonder if any of these men had taken part in the ambush and murders of her father and grandfather. On the other hand, she had complete confidence that none of them had been among those who had barged into their home later that morning. Those poor excuses for men had faces that would remain forever burned into her memory.

Often, her downcast eyes still managed to see little children, most with dirty, tear-stained faces. Some wandered aimlessly in the streets. Others merely sat, with blank eyes staring forward.

"God only knows what horrors these children have witnessed," Emine thought. She surmised that these children had been orphaned during the still ongoing Ottoman attack on the city of Van. Oh, how deeply she wished she could gather them to her and protect them. Down various side streets into the now well-barricaded Armenian quarter, she could hear the sounds of women and children crying, wailing, and whimpering. Hell had been brought to their doors.

She did not speak up. She did not break her stride. The group walked on and on, most purposefully away from the fighting.

Gunshots rang regularly in the distance. Both she and Halime jumped each and every time a cannon blasted. Still, they walked onward.

Once outside the city, Emine was about to learn a new lesson of carnage. First a putrid smell accosted her nose.

"I cannot breathe!" Halime clung tightly to Emine's arm as she barely whispered the words. The young woman fully understood and did her best to support the older woman. The stench in the air clung heavily to every breath they took.

Clarity brought the understanding that this was the smell of death. As they passed the rotting bodies of dead Armenians, the soldiers did not even blink. Emine's stomach retched, and she thought she might truly vomit.

The further from the city they got, the more evidence of massacres they saw. Women, children, and elderly. Sometimes the hacked bodies were in rows. Other times these poor people seemed to have been tossed in mounds. Often the women and girls had been stripped naked. Bodies were everywhere... under trees, along roadsides, and along the banks of creeks.

Had this been the fate of her mother, Aghavni Gulumian, little Hrant, and her sickly twin Vahram? Could their bodies truly be among those they were now passing? Emine pushed such thoughts and images from her mind.

Despite soldiers' reports that they had found and killed that Gulumian trio, Emine could not believe it. She *would* not believe it. Her mother would never have walked along the main roads. The plan had been to cross the meadows and pastures toward the north and then to cross their sacred Mount Ararat on a route to the safety of Kars in what was now the Russian Empire. Then again, one of the landmarks they would be seeking near the city of Van was a monastery. That indeed was along a road.

She had lost everything. Her family. Her home. Her city. Her beloved Toros.

There was no time to grieve. They hurried on toward the shipyard.

The Crossing

9

ARRIVING AT THE dock on Lake Van, Serkan tensed. The Armenian sailors had been safely transporting Turk and Armenian refugees across the lake. However, those refugees were civilians. Serkan was military. Though not in uniform, soldiers had arrived with the little group, and the soldiers were now unloading the foursome's scant parcels. This had surely not gone unnoticed.

Yavuz handed some coins to the sailor beside the gangway. No one sought papers of any sort. Refugees usually had no documentation anyway.

Carrying their little bundles, the nervous foursome boarded the boat. They all felt every eye onboard staring at them. Or were they just fearing that was so? They found a small open bench and sat down.

No conversation could be heard anywhere on the vessel. These were all nervous travelers, and this was not a pleasure cruise.

As more weary refugees continued to board, Emine let her thoughts wander as she gazed out across the seemingly endless water. She recalled so many wonderful times growing up on Lake Van at the Gulumian summer home by the orchards. Sleeping on the rooftop under the stars in the fresh air of summer nights reigned among her favorite memories.

Finally, the sailors skillfully maneuvered the vessel away from the harbor and out onto the open waters. Emine closed her eyes as she listened to the water slapping the sides of the boat. The crossing would be long, but it saved days of walking through dangerous territory to Bitlis.

She smiled as she recalled young Hrant singing gleefully and her sweet younger sister Anush telling stories and making everyone laugh during their summer outings. Fresh fruits and vegetables were bountiful here, and many friends came to visit to share meals or stay for a few days. Music, merriment, and laughter all flowed easily here. She knew she would always cherish the memories made at their Lake Van summer home.

Sweet thoughts ground to a halt. An Armenian man now spoke aloud in Turkish just off to the right of Serkan. His tone seethed with hatred and anger.

"YOU! You are one of THEM! And worse than that, you are an officer!"

As the man stood up, Serkan caught the glint of the knife the man was pulling from its sheath. Before he could protest, another Armenian intervened.

"Sir, please. Yes, I recognize him, also. Yes, he is an Ottoman officer. But he is also the man who helped my family into hiding when the other soldiers were slaughtering everyone in our village."

"Pshaw!" The first Armenian retorted. "One family against thousands murdered. That is not enough. He does not deserve to breathe the air around us!"

As he advanced toward Serkan, Emine knew she must break her silence... and her promise. There was no time to lose. Though traveling dressed as a Turkish woman, she immediately now spoke up loudly, without invitation, and in perfect Armenian.

"He saved my life!" All eyes immediately fell on Emine. Who was this Turkish woman who dared speak up so boldly? And in Armenian at that.

Her tone softened as she continued. "This man rescued me after the evil Ottoman soldiers repeatedly ravaged my sister and me, then shot us, leaving us for dead."

She had now fully captured the would-be attacker's attention. All murmuring and activity onboard ceased entirely. Everyone stared as she continued speaking.

"Yes, my sister was dead in our own home, but somehow, I survived. This man risked everything by taking me into his home where his wife has been caring for me for weeks now and helping me become well enough to travel... disguised as a Turk for my safety and theirs. They have been friends of my family for years. He is NOT like those beasts and should not be blamed for *their* evil behavior."

The man was listening. He was not advancing, but her words were not soothing his ire. "He is Ottoman military. HE is evil."

Now Emine's volume and pitch rose sharply. Though uncharacteristic for the usually even-tempered young woman, she did not hold back.

"NO! Evil Ottomans ambushed and murdered my Papa and Grandpapa just outside our city walls. Evil Ottomans entered our home and viciously attacked my sister and me. Evil Ottomans wounded my mother and forced her and my two brothers, who were disguised as young girls, into one of their hideous marches out of the city. THIS man told them they must escape, run, and hide. Alas, we fear they failed. But he tried to help!"

Emine now looked anxiously from passenger to passenger, hoping her words had found some compassionate ears. Another nearby Armenian man spoke first.

"You have a strong and spirited tongue for one so young. Where did you learn this manner and courage?"

"From my Papa."

Tears now filled her eyes as she remembered his gentle way of teaching and his frequent telling of parables and relating old Armenian proverbs. She knew that Papa would never have raised his voice, and she herself had been known for being quiet and sweet. She calmed her tone.

"Papa told us to be aware of evil. But he also reminded us that blame for the evil acts of *some* people should not be cast upon all *other* people. Proverbs he would share in this case might be 'One can spoil the good name of a thousand.' Or he might say, 'One bad deed begets another,' and then there is no victory for anyone."

The man who had spoken now tilted his hand up, indicating that she had said enough. He then asked, "If you do not mind me asking, what is your family name?"

"It is Gulumian. Papa is... Papa was a skillful tailor and merchant."

Another man spoke up now. "Ah, I knew your father Garabed well. Our prayers are with you. We heard what they did to him. And yet compassion remains in your heart."

Now the man still wielding his knife, returned the blade into its sheath. His tone relaxed.

He directly addressed Emine. "I am consumed with anger and pain. I do want revenge or justice or something. The only parable that entered my mind when you first spoke was 'The only sword that never rests is the tongue of a woman.' Yet now, I am glad you spoke. Your family has educated you well. If you can be somehow calm amidst all this hellacious chaos, I guess I can find it in my heart to give this Turkish soldier a chance, too. My apologies, sir, if I offended you."

Serkan Raffi knew enough Armenian language to understand the man's apology. And he managed to reply in the best Armenian words he could muster. He spoke softly as he said, "There is no apology needed. These are times well beyond severe for all of us. Sometimes I believe we all need to hear the calm wisdom of the young among us."

Emine lowered her face now. As she spoke again, she did so in Turkish. "I spoke without an invitation. It was not my place."

"Nonsense," replied Serkan. "You are educated, unlike most of us. And you were taught to think for yourself and to share those thoughts. I recall seeing this often through your mother.

"While that is difficult in Ottoman culture, it seems that we are among *your* people here, so no harm has been done. In many cultures, such candid expressions could bring dire consequences. But far be it for me to want anything more than your safety. And, after all, your ability to take a stand so directly just saved me from a nasty knife attack."

The remainder of the crossing passed without further incident. Emine found herself gazing out over the water again, hoping for even a fleeting glimpse of Akhtamar Island, but they had long ago passed it.

She remembered attending the elegant wedding ceremony there in the Cathedral of the Holy Cross. And then the incredibly festive reception held at their summer house.

Ahhhh... If Fate had been kinder, perhaps she would have enjoyed a similar day of love and laughter as she married Toros. She could still picture his handsomely chiseled face. She envisioned the way happiness exuded from his every pore when he elegantly danced the many Armenian dances he knew so well.

Emine closed her eyes again. She could not help but think that she did not feel brave at all. Her younger sister Anush had been the gutsy, spirited one. Anush was now gone.

Perhaps Nazeli was gone, too. Emine no longer felt like the young woman she was when she was called Nazeli... the one known as being sweet and gentle and soft-spoken. The time for tenderness and timidity had passed. There would be no more girlish giggling. Her strength and fortitude were being tested. Becoming a survivor appeared more than likely to be her destiny.

Unity
10

IN THE BEAUTIFUL flat in Knightsbridge, Nuray placed the papers from which she had just been reading into a folder. She closed the folder and placed it in front of her on the coffee table.

Silence softened the room for a few moments. Then Cassie spoke. "Thank you for sharing that with me. It is heartening to learn how difficult times could bring very different people together in a positive unity."

"Oh, yes," Sidika now commented. "'Unity is power,' as my mother used to say."

"Another Armenian proverb," Nuray smiled as she commented on her mother's response.

Cassie sought some additional clarification. "So, Sidika, did Nazeli... I mean Emine... end up truly marrying Yavuz? So, he became your father?"

Sidika shook her head. "Oh, no. That might have seemed like a good storybook ending. But I was not yet ready to be born. Life had a few more unforeseen turns coming. Let's share them over a spot of tea or some lunch at one of the lovely cafes that are very close by."

"Yes, of course," Cassie said. "Whatever you wish."

"Nuray, bring the next folder with us. Let's take Cassie to Al Basha. You will like it, Cassie. It's a short walk from here... right on Knightsbridge. They are Lebanese and serve a splendid variety of hot and cold appetizers."

Sidika was right, of course. They ordered items that included Tabbouleh, a chopped parsley, mint, onion, and tomato mixture tossed with cracked wheat, lemon juice, and olive oil. They also had Cassie try the grilled Halloumi cheese, along with some sujuk, which are spicy Lebanese sausages fried with tomato and diced onion in a light chili sauce. As if that wasn't enough, they shared some tasty pastry triangles filled with spinach, onion, and sumac, which delivered a perfect citrusy zest, and the Arab-inspired kafta skewers of minced lamb with onions and chopped parsley, served with rice.

The delectable items the ladies were sharing started to be delivered in succession. Cassie's hunger, however, was not for the yummy foods.

"Everything is utterly delicious, but can you give me a hint of what you will be serving up from inside this next folder?" Cassie gestured toward the folder sitting on the table beside Nuray.

"Well, I could, of course," came Sidika's reply. "However, that would spoil *my* mother's enormous surprise."

Sidika smiled, as Cassie raised her eyebrows. Nuray then opened the folder and removed the next group of carefully prepared pages as she simply said, "This could be a bumpy ride. Ladies, fasten your seatbelts."

Constantinople

11

DAYS ON THE road were long, but fortunately, uneventful. Emine's gunshot wound seemed to have healed almost completely. Traveling including many hours of quiet time, which the teen used to think... to process all that had been happening. Barely three months had passed since that fateful day when her world began to unravel.

They had since learned that the Russians did arrive in time to save the Armenians, just before they ran out of ammunition in fact. The Ottomans were deeply angered to learn that the Russian soldiers found the exhausted ranks of Armenians singing while still sitting in their trenches in the walled city of Van. Singing! They were singing songs of Armenian patriotism and tradition.

This news made Emine smile. And there was more. A new Armenian republic in the Van province was announced, and their family friend, Aram Manukian had been named Governor. She could hardly believe it.

They had done it! For the first time the Armenians had stood up to the Ottoman government and succeeded. She so wished her father could have lived to see this.

The cost was high. Many lives were lost to both military actions and massacres. But at this moment in time, the Armenians had won. They had withstood the weeks of cannon fire barrage. The Ottoman Army had withdrawn completely, causing many more Turkish civilians to join the Armenians as refugees.

Now in Constantinople, Serkan Raffi gathered his weary travelers. His smile was genuine.

"We have made it," he began. "You have all been wonderful and strong throughout this difficult journey. Please remember that our little ruse must continue here. Though we are in a quarter with many Armenians, Nazeli must remain Emine, speaking only Turkish and practicing Turkish decorum.

He turned to Emine specifically now. "We will be living with our son, Aydin. He is the only other person who knows who you really are. You probably remember him from being children together."

Emine nodded. How could she possibly forget that funny little boy. Aydin and her older brother Aram had been close friends. She'd even had a crush on him when they were children.

She had not seen Aydin in years, but she knew he had suffered great personal tragedy when he lost both his wife and unborn baby, as she struggled through an impossible birth. Understandably, he had withdrawn socially after that. She had no idea what he would be like as an adult.

She did not have long to wait. Before she knew it, they were at his door.

"Welcome, Father! I have missed you, too, dearest Mother!" Aydin seemed effervescent. Hugs were exchanged, each one meaningful and long overdue.

Halime wept tears of joy. Aydin kept one arm around her as he greeted Yavuz.

"Well, Cousin, welcome home. And aren't you the lucky one!?! Your bride is the lovely Nazeli... excuse me, I mean Emine."

Emine lowered her face and was certain her cheeks were flushed with red. He did remember her after all.

"No Aydin," Yavuz immediately spoke up. "This is merely a ruse. We are not and will not be wed. She has not given up her Christianity, and your father insists that is her choice. I will only wed a proper Muslim woman, and not some Pagan."

"Yavuz!" Serkan sounded shocked. "That is no way to speak."

"Uncle Serkan, you knew my position when we started this deception. I apologize, but I did not previously understand that you meant for it to continue after we got here to Constantinople."

Emine had not raised her face. Her girlish flush of utter embarrassment had suddenly changed to disappointment and anger. Yavuz had always been stern, but he had also seemed to treat her with kindness. Now she knew he merely saw her as an inconveniently heavy burden.

"Woah, family!" Aydin interrupted before the exchange of words became more heated.

"I appreciate seeing you all. You are my family. It is good to see you, too, young lady. As your brother, my dear friend Aram Gulumian used to remind me, 'A guest belongs to God.' You are all welcome here, regardless of religion."

With that he shot a brief, but scowling side glance at his cousin. He then looked to see Emine's reaction.

She ever so slowly looked up now, hoping her disappointment did now show. She was grateful to see genuine kindness in Aydin's eyes.

"Thank you for your hospitality and safe haven," she sincerely said to Aydin. "I am grateful to your parents for all they have done and risked rescuing and hiding me. I am grateful to you, too, Yavuz. And I apologize, as I did not mean to be such a great burden on you."

"I did not mean for it to sound that way," snapped Yavuz. He briefly pinched his eyelids together, sighed, and softened his tone. "Please understand that I also was to be married. I lost my fiancée, too. Illness took her from me before we could be wed, but I dream of getting married and having a family... a Turkish Muslim family. If you convert to Islam, I will gladly marry you in real life."

The room grew silent for a few moments. Emine did not know what to say. She felt as if he were talking about her like an object to bid on at the bazaar.

So, this was to be her future? How was she expected to breathe?

Emine closed her eyes, but her thoughts screamed in her brain. "Oh, Toros!!! Toros! Toros! I miss you so much."

Serkan stepped in to calm the situation. "I think we are all very weary after so many stressful days of travel. Perhaps we can have a calm evening and see the world in a brighter light after a night's rest."

"Yes! Excellent idea." Aydin smiled. "I have food prepared. Come. We will wash our hands and dine now. Afterward we men will smoke and talk and catch up on too much lost time."

The men turned and left the room. Halime moved immediately to Emine.

"I am sorry, my dear. I fear this cultural adaptation may be more challenging for you than we may have first thought. Come. You and I will go into the kitchen, and I will make us some tea. When the men finish, we will eat a bite ourselves and then get you settled in to sleep."

The room seemed to spin. Emine was so tired she felt dizzy. Life was taking some crazy turns. Would she convert to Islam? Could she? Just to get married to this stern man she did not love and was not sure she could grow to love? Well, would it have been so different in a traditional Armenian arranged marriage to someone other than her Toros?

Papa always said, "In a town, if you observe that people wear the hat on one side, wear yours likewise." So, she was wearing the headscarf and learning proper behavior for both inside and outside a Muslim home.

The warmth of a cup of tea sounded good. Tomorrow was another day.

Reckoning

12

HALIME WALKED INTO the kitchen to prepare morning coffee. Huddled in one corner of the room was Emine. She rushed to lass.

"Emine! Emine! Are you alright?"

"Oh, Aunt Halime," the young woman gushed. "I fear this was all a mistake. I never should have come. I have caused too much angst for your family already. I think I am going to run away now, but I do not have a clue where I might go. I wish I had just died along with Anush back at our home in Van!"

Now she was completely awash in tears. The elder woman wrapped her arms around Emine and gently rocked her.

"Shhhh. Shhhh. Everything will be alright. You will be alright. Shhhh." In the early morning light, they sat like this for several minutes before Halime spoke again.

"I know this is all very traumatic for you, my dear," she began. "I am here for you. So is Uncle Serkan. We will help you grieve. We will help you learn. We will help you grow more comfortable in this new world. It is not so bad, truly."

Emine forced a meek smile. Halime had truly been wonderful to her, and Emine did not know what she would have done without her.

"I have felt very sick this morning, Aunt Halime. I did not eat anything bad last evening. In truth, I have had the same queasiness in my stomach for several days. Worse than that, I cannot stop this dizziness."

Halime smiled warmly and brushed a stray lock of hair off Emine's beautiful, tear-streaked face. "Oh, my dear, I am sorry. You are probably just very overtired from all the travel."

"She's not just overtired," came a male voice from across the room. Aydin had slipped into the kitchen and simply stopped inside the doorway when he saw the two women sitting on the floor talking.

"Of course, she is, Aydin. On top of that she is dealing with a great deal of stress, anxiety, and grief."

"Mama, have you stopped to consider any other possibility?" Ayden now helped both women up off the floor and into chairs.

Emine felt mortified. Here she hadn't seen Ayden in years, and she had completely come unwound in his kitchen.

Halime tilted her head to the side. He continued.

"When my wife was first with child, she suffered nausea and vomiting and a great deal of dizziness. She also had a few overly... emotional breakdowns."

Emine turned quickly to face Halime. She shook her head rapidly.

"No," she protested. "This could not be possible. I have not married. I have not bedded a man."

Halime reached out to Emine and took both her hands in her own. She sighed deeply.

"Oh, my sweet girl. You have not bedded a man... by choice. But when you and your sister were attacked, you were... ravaged, correct?"

Emine nodded. She also realized that months had passed without her monthly visitor.

"I believe it was three different soldiers who disrespected you. I am sorry, but that means that you could indeed have been impregnated by any one of them."

"Oh, nooooooo!" Emine released a slow and painfully soft wail of disdainful reckoning.

Quandary

13

INDEED, EMINE WAS pregnant. She imagined that she should have known because her belly had been thickening in recent weeks. Now it did not matter if she would or would not choose to convert to Islam. She was going to give birth to a baby in just a few months.

"I know that I said I would marry you if you converted to Islam," Yavuz began. "But this... this baby is different. This changes everything. Again, I mean no personal insult, but I do not wish to marry a woman who is carrying some other man's baby, even if the man is a Turk. I realize that this situation was not your choice. But marrying a pregnant woman would not be my choice either."

Yavuz continued without hesitation. "On the other hand, I gave my word, and I would be no sort of man if I did not honor my word. So, *if* you convert, you can count on me to keep my word. Only you, Emine, and Uncle Serkan, of course, can release me from my promise."

Emine sat numbly, staring into space. Halime sat beside her, holding her hand on the table before them. Serkan and Yavuz sat across from them. Aydin stood behind the women, leaning on the wall listening, but not taking part in the conversation.

Her family was gone. Her fiancé was gone. Her eldest brothers were somewhere in America. For all intent and purposes, Serkan had become the head of the household for her. In theory and by tradition that meant that he could arrange for her marriage. But traditions... both Armenian and Ottoman... were getting all jumbled up here.

"What are *your* thoughts, Emine," Serkan asked softly. She hardly knew what she might say. Did they all think she could somehow make such a decision sitting at this table in this very moment?

"This is a very big decision," she hesitantly began. "Quite frankly, I am rather frightened. I do not fancy going through this alone. And yet, I also appreciate your... reluctance, Yavuz, to be strapped with... me, never mind a baby, too. Is it possible for me to take a few hours to think this over?"

Serkan glanced at everyone at the table. "Of course, you can take some time to think the situation through. This impacts more than just one life. You are a very smart and educated young woman. You will come to the best decision, I am sure. Let us say that we will talk again tonight, after dinner. There a decision will be made."

Everyone nodded in agreement. Yavuz stood first. As he turned from the table toward the door, he slowly shook his head, feeling his fate... his future... was completely out of his hands.

Serkan stood next. He motioned for his wife to join him. Halime rose, her face filled with concern as she looked back at Emine as they left the room.

Aydin watched his young friend for a few moments before speaking. How could one young woman survive all that she had only to have to face yet another trauma?

He quietly and calmly began. "Emine, there is a lovely, walled garden in my back yard. When I need time to think, I have often found great peace and inspiration there. Please, let me show you."

Her back was still toward him where she sat at the table. She paused, but then nodded her head. Aydin walked around to face her. He held out his hand, inviting her to take it.

The moment they stepped into the garden, she smiled. Yes, she could understand why this peaceful setting could clear one's mind. Along one wall, healthy vines grew, and they were filled with an abundance of pink flowers. Several large, decorative urns sat, artistically arranged amidst various neatly groomed and blossoming shrubs. A tidy stone pathway curved toward a beautiful bench under a tree that was very reminiscent of the mulberry tree she had enjoyed in her family's own walled yard.

Yes, this was the perfect place to ponder her future and how today's decision would affect it. She turned to Aydin and smiled.

"This is most kind of you. It reminds me of home, where I can picture my brother Aram and you sitting in the walled garden in the evenings, sharing a smoke and reading books by torch light."

"Ahhh, you remember all the reading." Aydin laughed. "You would not realize this, but it was your brother who inspired me to seek education, rather than following my father into a military career. Now, thanks in great part to that education, I am a well-respected man of business. Moving here has served me very well financially. Since this city was first settled in the 7th century BC, the port has thrived due to its prime geographic location between Europe and Asia."

Aydin now walked a bit away from her, staring at the various flowers around him. He then began to speak again without facing her.

"On the fateful night when my wife and baby died during the difficult delivery, this is where I sought solace. She planted many of these flowers and had tended to them lovingly. Under the stars that night, I felt she was still very much with me." Now he turned to face Emine. He nodded his head as he approached.

"Though years have passed, her strength is still here, Emine." He continued. "Let her help you as she did me. My father wants what is best for you... and your baby. You know that in our culture, because the father is Turkish, so is the baby. Yavuz will come around. I know he can seem very rigid and curt, but he is a good person. His heart is true."

Emine sat on the bench. She took in the delicate beauty all around her.

"Aydin, may I ask you a question?" She paused awaiting his answer.

"Of course, you can, sweet Emine. Anything."

"Why did you not marry again?"

Aydin did not turn away. And yet, his eyes cast downward as he pondered his words.

"Under the stars that night I realized I had lost the start of my own family. Childbirth can be dangerous, yes, but she was strong and healthy. I could not fathom why this had happened to her... to us. Then I felt the answer come to me. This was the will of Allah. He must have had other plans for me."

Emine remembered Aydin well from her youth. His personality was vibrant. He was handsome, smart, and hardworking. How could she have not had a childhood crush on him, even though he was not Christian? Now she felt very sad for him.

"So, what did you do? How did you cope with feeling so much grief and emptiness?"

He smiled the slightest of wry smiles. Then he nodded as he continued.

"I buried myself in my work. Truly, I became obsessive about it. It seems that I became quite skillful at brokering deals for both imports and exports... all sorts of goods, from pepper and cocoa to tobacco and silver. While I built up a great reputation and wealth, all that was important to me was gone. I admit that I detached myself from everyone else. I worked. I prayed. That has been all."

"I am deeply sorry for your suffering," was all that Emine could think of saying. And yet, she added, "I know that your father and mother have missed you terribly."

"Yes, cutting myself off from life was not likely my best option." Aydin continued. "I lost my family and friends from Van. I lost your brother, Aram. I lost myself. That is why I want you to think carefully. Close your eyes. Pray. The guidance will come to you. We will all talk again after dinner."

With that, Aydin walked back inside. He left a heavy air of sadness. Like herself, he had lost everything that mattered to him. Though he could earn money, she knew that being alone had been difficult for him.

She had never been alone. Never. However, in the next few hours of thought and reflection, Emine did not shed a tear. She recognized that she had taken the strength and vitality of her family very much for granted. The treasure of her beloved family had now been yanked from under her feet, and she would have done anything to bring it all back.

Perhaps this was her path now to follow. Maybe this was her opportunity to set herself aside. She could teach the value of family, love, and loyalty to this unborn child growing within her... and somehow also to a man that would be scheduled to become her husband.

Emine shuddered. Could she handle this? She said another prayer for strength before reentering the house to learn her new destiny.

Decision Time

14

THE MEN HAD dined rather quickly, without the usual frivolity. When they headed out into the garden to smoke, Emine and Halime sat at the table.

"You need to eat," Halime said matter-of-factly. She pushed a platter with kebabs and vegetables toward the young woman.

Emine shook her head. "I am simply not hungry."

"Ah, that is not a surprise to hear, especially considering how... how challenging the world has become for you," Halime said nodding. She then began transferring a few food items to Emine's plate.

"You may not feel hunger, but you must eat anyway. The little one inside you is hungry. You are bringing a new member to our family. We want to do everything we can to keep you and the baby healthy."

"What? You would consider my baby to be your family?" Emine was genuinely surprised.

Halime gestured for Emine to put some food into her mouth. She waited for her to do so before speaking.

"My dear child, when we brought you into our home, we already felt you were like family. We had all been friends for your entire life. Now... with your own birth family gone, we are honored to become your new family. You are like a niece. Any child of yours will be our great nephew... or great niece. How could you ever imagine that we would abandon you now?"

Emine swallowed the bite she was chewing. Then she shared a rather bittersweet smile.

"I guess I had not thought it through that way. Sadness is all I have been able to feel lately. I never imagined anyone else would ever consider me as their family."

Emine put down the piece of bread she was holding and continued. "And you have taken me in though I am Christian."

Halime smiled. She understood. "My dear, our religious and cultural differences have never kept us apart. Your family always respected us during our month of Ramadan. And our family always visited you during your Christmas holidays. Friendship, trust, and respect bring us together. Only focusing on differences tears us apart."

"Thank you... Aunt Halime." Emine was about to speak again, but the men entered the room. The elder woman continued to sit beside Emine and held her hand as the men took their seats.

Her new Uncle Serkan sat directly across from Emine, with his nephew Yavuz on his left. Serkan's son Aydin, their host, remained standing off to the side of the table.

Silence hovered for a few moments. Emine kept her gaze on the table, not daring to look up even at Serkan. At long last, Serkan cleared his throat and began.

"My dear Emine, I know these last few days have been especially difficult for you. And now, my nephew Yavuz has expressed his willingness to follow my plan and marry you. However, it is his wish... his preference that you convert to Islam. Do you understand that this is not my requirement, but his wish?"

She nodded. However, it was a wish with which she did not want to comply. Her faith was strong, and she knew that only force could make her convert.

Serkan continued. "As a Christian, you believe in the Holy Trinity, and you call Jesus, the Christ, the son of God. Your churches contain a great many statues while we do not believe in idolatry. That said, as Muslims, we believe that your Jesus was one of the prophets who revealed Allah's word... God's word. And we believe he was a great prophet who performed miracles. Also, both Christians and Muslims believe that we are all the children of Allah. And we believe in the afterlife.

"If you agree to convert to Islam, our society will welcome you and protect you. If you do not convert, our family will still welcome you and protect you, but you will have to behave as a Muslim woman and practice our traditions anyway. Emine, do you understand?"

She nodded her head, keeping her gaze down. "Yes, Uncle Serkan, I do."

"Then, please, dear girl. Please look at me."

Emine slowly raised her face to look at Serkan. His eyes were soft and gentle, but his mouth was firmly set.

"You have had time to ponder your future. Are you ready to share your decision with us now?

Emine took some time to look at each person at the table. She took a deep breath.

"Perhaps you would permit me to speak before she does," interrupted Yavuz. "My apologies, Uncle, but I may have another solution. One that may be more acceptable to everyone."

Alternatives

15

ALL EYES NOW focused on Yavuz. What possible alternative proposal was he thinking?

"Perhaps your conversion is unnecessary, because perhaps a wedding is not needed." Yavuz continued. "We can bring in a midwife at this early stage. I understand they have potions that can take away this... er, problem."

Serkan spoke immediately. "Yes, this is done in some circles. However, it is highly discouraged."

"Discouraged, yes, Uncle. But not against the law! And she is just a Christian, after all."

Now Serkan's tone took on a stern tone. "Yavuz, even a pregnant Christian woman has rights. You also fail to mention that these potions often pose a deep threat to the expectant mother!"

The two men stared determinedly at each other. No one saw the tears that now trickled down Emine's face.

Though she had not expressed her thoughts when Serkan had first asked if she was ready to share her decision. Now, without any further invitation, she began to speak.

"I believe I have caused enough angst in this family. I have placed you all at risk of discovery for harboring a Christian. And now I am with child."

At this point, Emine looked up at Serkan before continuing. "Please know that I mean you no disrespect, Uncle Serkan, when I tell you now that I will not willingly convert to Islam. My faith is all I have left, and despite commonalities between our religions, I will not denounce mine.

"Nor will I accept this new... 'solution' for the baby I unwittingly carry. Still, if you insist on arranging a marriage to your nephew, I will comply. Or, if you choose to cast me out on the street, I will understand that also. You and your entire family will always have my gratitude for saving my life."

She looked back down at the table. Unseen by the men, Halime gave her hand a squeeze.

"Oh, Emine," Serkan began slowly. "You put me in a most difficult situation."

At this point, Aydin took one step toward the table. "Father, if I may be so bold, perhaps I may be allowed to speak."

"You are our host, son," replied Serkan. "Of course, we would all deeply value any insight you may offer."

"Thank you, Father." Now Aydin looked at his cousin.

"Yavuz, not all that long ago, you were set to marry a woman you had not even met, never mind grown to care for yet. However, and I am grateful for this, you do not know the pain of losing a wife you loved, nor the pain of losing a child."

Aydin glanced at Emine before continuing. "I have known this young woman since she was a child. And Father, I believe that if my cousin knew her, he would be standing in line for the opportunity to marry her. Yes, even with a baby. And yes, despite religious differences.

"I can attest to her intelligence, loyalty, sweet and gentle personality, and her outstanding home skills. She is a wonderful cook and can sew anything you could ever want. I have also seen her interact beautifully with children.

"Plus, I knew her parents and how she and her siblings were raised. No man could ever ask for a more dedicated or beautiful woman to make his wife... and mother for his children... and any children."

Now there was a pause. Serkan turned to look at his nephew. The eyebrows on the young man's face were furrowed. Yavuz stood before speaking.

"Well... dear... cousin... Aydin," Yavuz began slowly. "That was quite a powerful testimony for a woman you have not seen for at least 3 or 4 years. If you believe that she is so wonderful, perhaps your father will release me from my promise to marry her, and let *you* marry her."

"And, if he did release you from your promise, Yavuz, I would earnestly plead for that opportunity."

Yavuz' jaw dropped. Aydin continued, as he began to walk around, passing first behind Ermine, who still sat with her face down toward the table.

"When my wife and unborn child died, I thought my life was gone, too. Over. Done. I was crushed. My dreams were shattered. I buried myself in my work in my attempts to escape from the world. Slowly... ever so slowly, my grief turned to sadness, and from my loneliness grew a peculiar sort of acceptance. I learned to believe that somehow, I would learn to dream a new dream."

Now he stopped directly across from Emine and behind his father. He placed his right hand on Serkan's shoulder.

"Father, please forgive my insolence. And Emine, please do me the honor of looking at me now." She raised her eyes to meet his sincere gaze.

"When I first learned that my mother and father were coming here and bringing you, I felt something delightful... something that I had not sensed in years. It was as if my heart gave a happy little jump. I felt a lightness... a brightness filled the room... a room that had felt shrouded in darkness for too long.

"Though I knew that my cousin Yavuz traveled with you and was to become married to you, I especially looked forward to seeing you again. And I was not disappointed. If possible, you have grown into an even more beautiful young woman.

"Though it was never my intention to challenge my father's wishes for you, Emine, perhaps I can now offer an even better solution to this challenging situation.

"Father... Yavuz... it would be my honor to marry Emine and become a father for her unborn child. I will promise to both love and honor you, Emine, and your son or daughter, as if the baby were truly my own."

Now Yavuz sat back down and looked at his Uncle Serkan with renewed hope in his eyes. Aydin stepped back to the side of the table where he had first stood when this conversation began, but he never took his eyes off Emine. Her eyes also stayed locked on his as he moved.

Serkan looked first at Yavuz. Seeing the excitement on his face, he then looked at his son. Aydin looked caring and compassionate.

Turning toward his wife, Serkan saw the hope on her face. He could also clearly see that his son and Emine had a natural connection. Halime now held Emine's right hand tightly wrapped in both her hands and pressed to her heart.

"Well, family," Serkan began. "We have all been through some strange and horrific times. Everything else is out of the ordinary, so why should this situation be anything other than utterly nontraditional?"

Turning now to Yavuz, Serkan nodded. "Yes, you are released from your promise to marry Emine. And I agree with my son that this is indeed your loss."

Next, he looked at Emine. "So, young lady, do you need more time to consider marrying my son, Aydin?"

"Not even one minute," she answered simply. "I would be honored."

Together

16

A LOCAL IMAM performed the Nikah, the Islamic wedding ceremony, and they obtained the official marriage certificate from the government. Everything was legal because a Muslim man is permitted to marry a Christian woman.

Aydin had kept his word. They were married, and she remained a Christian. That does not mean that he did not try.

"I have told Allah how I feel about you," Aydin said one day. "I open my heart to Him in my daily prayers. Dear Emine, I want you to go with me to heaven, and I already know you put God first in your life. Is there a chance that you would be willing to attend a mosque to perhaps better understand Islam?"

Emine sweetly smiled at her new husband. "Dearest Aydin, there is little you might ask me that I would not do. You have been true to your word. You always treat me with kindness, just as you promised. Also, as you promised, you never raise your voice in anger to me, and I feel no fear. I know you are always there to protect me.

"You also know that I promised to uphold the Muslim requirement that children born into a mixed marriage must be raised in Islam and with all Muslim traditions and practices in our home. I will be honored to attend your mosque."

Aydin gently kissed her on the forehead. "There is no compulsion to religion in Islam, but Mother will also be so pleased. She will feel honored to have you with her as the ladies pray."

Emine attended the mosque, but she did not convert to Islam. With Halime's daily assistance, she created a loving home filled with Muslim tradition.

The months passed quickly. Soon it was her time to deliver the baby.

"Please do not be too nervous," Emine spoke sincerely to Aydin. "I am healthy, but I know the childbirth event brings back traumatic memories for you. And whatever happens is God's will... Allah's will. I know that you will not let this child be orphaned."

Aydin pulled her close to him. "You will be right here with me raising *our* baby. Yes, I know the father was a sinfully cruel, ill-behaving Turkish soldier. I remind myself that he was like so many others, sadly accepting the Young Turks' indoctrination. So many have accepted the lies and started believing that they commit no sin with their ongoing malicious deeds, because Armenians, Greeks... all Christians are somehow sub-human.

"Regardless, this baby... our baby... brought about by violence, will be raised in a loving home with a mother *and* father who will give unconditional love. Always."

Emine smiled again, but this time with a bit of a twist on her lips. Then she replied.

"I know that dear, and I appreciate your huge heart more than you can imagine. I also know that if a baby has Turkish blood, you consider him or her to be Turkish. We Armenians have similar sentiments. If you have even one drop of *Armenian* blood in you, then we consider you to be an Armenian. Sometimes I wonder just how many people who consider themselves to be Turkish are also Armenians."

"Hah!" Aydin laughed. "The Ottomans would not want to hear you say that! Centuries ago, when their troops first started arriving here in the West and in Anatolia by your sacred Mount Ararat, a great many babies were created.

"Many scholars acknowledge that this included very deliberate actions to have babies with the beautiful Armenian women to help mellow the old Mongolian appearance. And yet, no one ever stopped to consider that all those many thousands of offspring had Armenian blood. Even our Sultans have chosen Christians and other Caucasians to be mothers for their children. By this point in time, our similarities far outnumber our differences."

"Hmmm... someone should tell that to the government." Emine sighed.

And then she winced. Her water broke and her labor pains began.

The Birthing
17

THE JEWISH MIDWIFE arrived with the birthing chair. Halime helped her with all the preparations. With each contraction, Emine looked to her mother-in-law for assurance.

"Yes, dear," Halime began. "Everything is going smoothly. Remember all that we have discussed. You are doing just fine."

Per the tradition of the times, Emine had stayed out of the public eye throughout her pregnancy. She became especially fond of the walled garden with all its colorful flowers and shady sitting areas.

Aydin proved to be the perfect husband. He doted on her every whim and wish. His decency and unselfishness were beyond compare, and her gratitude grew.

"How could I not grow to love this wonderful man?" Emine found herself thinking rather often. And yet, she had known her beloved fiancé Toros even longer than Aydin.

Or had she? Though Aydin's family was Muslim, he had been with her brother Aram very frequently, except during meetings regarding Armenian resistance planning, of course.

Toros had come from a family that was also very close to her own. Like her father, his own father had been a merchant. So, he had been around family gatherings since she could remember. His death still tugged at her heartstrings.

Aydin had also known Toros. He knew the loss was still very recent for Emine, and she appreciated his sensitivity.

"Emine," he had softly said. "I know you were in love with your fiancé, Toros. He was a wonderful young man... handsome, talented, and very witty. And his smile? Well, he could charm anyone out of anything. I liked him very much, too.

"Having lost my own wife, I appreciate the deeply empty place in your heart. Toros will always hold that place. I do not expect to fill it. My hope is that I can warm a new place in your heart, as you have in mine.

"And yet, I have had much longer than you have had to adjust to my lost love. Please know that I have profound patience. I put no time limit on opening your heart."

Emine would always cherish Aydin's kindness, composure, and his gentle manner with her. Surely, she would grow to love him. She already liked him very much.

For now, however, she focused on delivering this BABYYYYY! Another contraction. After several hours, she was exhausted, but Emine pushed hard again with all the might she could muster.

Success! Relief!

"Wa-a-a-a-a-a!" The baby's first cry was a highly welcomed sound.

Halime mopped her now daughter-in-law's brow with a moist towel. Emine was glad to see her broad smile. That was a good sign that things went well.

The midwife had caught the baby perfectly. She also submerged the newborn baby in a salty bath for the traditional Muslim cleansing and to help make the newborn resistant to evil.

When the midwife cut the umbilical cord, Halime found herself wondering out loud. "Where might my son choose to bury the umbilical cord?"

"What do you mean?" Emine weakly asked. Halime realized she had spoken her thoughts.

"Well, my dear," she began. "If buried in the yard of a mosque, the child will be an imam. If it is buried in a school yard, the child will become a teacher. Do you understand?"

Emine nodded her head before speaking. "Am I to gather from this that my baby is a boy?"

"Oh! Yes!" Halime almost laughed out loud.

"I got so involved that I forgot to tell you. Yes! You have a baby boy! And we have a grandson!"

"And he looks perfect," added the midwife. Now she dutifully washed the baby's mouth with honey. This tradition was meant to ensure that the child's speech would be sweet and beautiful.

Halime then hurried to the courtyard, where her son had been nervously awaiting news. They returned together without delay, and he rushed to Emine's side.

Immediately, Aydin knelt to whisper in the newborn's ear. In true Islamic tradition after a birth, he recited the adhan, the call to prayer, to his baby son.

For Emine, it did not go unnoticed how openly he had wept when the midwife reported that both mother and baby were doing beautifully. Emine cried with him. She recognized and was grateful that she was able to give him this much-needed experience to help his heart continue healing from his own earlier loss.

He gently kissed Emine's face all over, which made her laugh. Aydin then began to speak rapidly.

"I have thought so much about what our baby's name should be. I have asked Allah for guidance in my prayers each day. And we have a boy. I feel greatly honored.

"I have considered the meanings of many names. I like Adlee, which in Turkish means 'just' or 'fair.' It is Biblical, meaning 'one who is judged by God.' I also like the name Onur, because it denotes righteousness, integrity, and morality. Then again, Tanju is worthy of consideration since it means 'one who is blessed by Allah.'

"For tradition I thought we might combine the name of my father with the name of your father. However, while my father's name Serkan would be accepted, I feared that Garabed, the Armenian name of your father, could cause problems for a Muslim boy as he grew.

"So, I then thought about the fact that many of our Turkish boys' names end with 'an,' as do some Armenian boys' names.... Names like Savan and Vahan. There are also names that are very similar in our cultures.

"A favorite for me is the name of my dear friend... your brother... Aram. In Turkish it is quite similar... Arat. And then he would always remind us of my friend... and your family. But Emine, would any of these names be more or less important to you?"

She appreciated how often Aydin consulted her opinions on daily matters. But including her in naming the baby was extraordinary and outside his cultural norms. She knew his question was sincere, and she responded.

"Well, while perhaps difficult because it would be a constant reminder of how this child was conceived, Adlee may be appropriate to consider. I want no one to judge this innocent baby."

Emine continued. "I also like that you are not trying to eliminate my culture, while being sensitive to any potential challenges a boy may face growing up with any name that sounds Christian. Honoring your father would also be important. Aydin, I trust you to name this boy with care and sincerity."

"This boy," Aydin began slowly. "This boy is our son. You may call him *your* son, *my* son, or *our* son. Believe me when I assure you that I will be doing the same.

"The time will come when we tell him about his... er, history. However, we will speak to no one else of this. And we will take great care to help him always know that he is loved and valued, not just as our first-born, but as our son."

A tear spilled down Emine's cheek as she listened to her husband speak. She could barely respond, which she finally did quite simply.

"Thank you, Aydin."

"Let me see... I agree with you on the name Adlee. That holds great promise in its meaning and shows our faith that only Allah... only God can judge. And I like letting my friend and your brother Aram become a connection to your heritage, but with Arat being our Turkish approach. Another name with great meaning is Berat, which in Turkish means..."

"Means the night of forgiveness," Emine interjected.

They both smiled. Then Aydin continued.

"My dear, I simply adore your intelligence and education. You know, there are those who have often quipped that the Armenians are illiterate for the most part. How very angry they would be to have to accept that your people not only valued educating boys, but also the girls. I am afraid it is we Turks who are arriving late to the education table."

Emine now responded, "Perhaps the Ottomans feared what would happen if the common people became educated. It is far easier for political groups to criticize others with the very words that should be used on themselves. Imagine the cultural shock when the masses finally learn how many great universities exist in other parts of the world, but not here at home."

"That is very observant, my dear." Aydin continued. "Our children will always learn the value of going to school. They will not be laborers or military, unless they choose to be.

"We will be certain to educate them in the best places we can. So, my brilliantly educated wife, would you be willing for us to name our child in a manner that is both traditional and yet, far outside customary?

Emine nodded. "Of course." Aydin now flashed the widest smile she had ever seen.

"What if we name him not just for friends and not just to honor family? I am thinking of Adlee, reflecting the fact that only Allah can judge, and Berat, meaning the night of forgiveness. I believe we will name our son Adlee Berat Raffi."

"Adlee Berat Raffi." Emine smiled. "It sounds wonderful."

News from Van
18

MEANWHILE, SERKAN HAD arrived home from his travels back to Anatolia. Upon hearing the news, he promptly retrieved the ritual clove sherbet that Halime had made in preparation for the birth. The refreshing beverage, made from cherries, plums, lemon juice, cinnamon, and cloves, was poured into a jug.

Leaving the jug open indicated that their new baby was a boy. Neighbors and friends would partake as they came to call.

He pulled his son aside to converse without the women hearing. He shook his head sadly.

"Aydin, what we found in the Van province was far worse than we had heard through reports. Before we departed to start our journey here to you in Constantinople, we knew the ancient walled city had been cut off from the Gardens. The Armenians within the walls were trying to defend their quarter there, while another 30,000 or so were crammed in a small district of only about 1 square mile in the Gardens.

"They had some 80 manned and barricaded homes, along with a few walls and trenches, but these were mostly civilians... women and children. They had less than 300 rifles, but somehow, they managed to withstand the massive Ottoman military onslaught, both within the walled city and in the Gardens.

"It turns out they had sent a manifest to the Turkish soldiers, explaining that their quarrel was with only one man... Governor Djevdet Bey. The Armenians got it right. They said that governors will come and go, but Turks and Armenians need to live together."

Aydin now asked, "Isn't the Van governor also the brother-in-law of Enver Pasha, the Minister of War?"

"Yes, and he is the one who insisted that the minority population must be eradicated. What he failed to note is that we Turks were the minority population in Van.

"The governor kept repeating that he had to put down the Armenian rebellion, although there was no rebellion. We lived there. We know the truth. Turks and Armenians had lived peacefully together throughout Van for many years. But he had proven repeatedly to the Armenians that he could not be trusted."

"Father," Aydin queried. "Were there some specific incidents that can stand as evidence of this?"

"Oh, yes, my son," came Serkan's immediate reply. "For example, the governor had asked some Armenian leaders to go as peace commissioners to the Shadakh region to ease troubles there. But he never had any intentions of having these men help.

"Those of us who were officers both saw and heard his orders. The governor ordered the soldiers to murder them all as soon as they were away from the city.

He merely wanted to remove some respected Armenian leaders from Van's potential resistance."

Aydin nodded with understanding as he replied. "Well, it makes sense then that the Armenians in Van had good reason to not trust him. My heart aches when I picture a cannon up on Castle Rock above the walled city simply bombarding the homes below with cannonballs. How on earth did anyone survive?"

"I do not know, son. Only by Allah's blessing. I am told that houses were burning in every direction. And the American compound in the Gardens district was not immune from destruction either."

"But Papa, we heard that the Russian army arrived and helped the Armenians." Aydin felt confused.

"You are right again, son," replied Serkan. "They came to the Armenians' relief just in time. However, the peace was short-lived. Once the Russians departed to go fight battles on other fronts, we Turks came in hard and fast. After killing thousands of civilians, almost everyone left in Van who had not successfully run away, we then destroyed every single building. And I mean every building, even the oldest stone churches, businesses, and homes."

"What? Van was a vibrant and beautiful city. This seems totally irrational."

"Though I served nearly my entire life in the Ottoman military, I must agree with you on this point. Let me take it one step further. What we are doing to the Armenian people makes no sense either. It goes way beyond inhumane and heartbreaking. I fear our leaders are no longer merely desperate. They have gone mad. And now, we are consciously destroying a 3,000-year-old civilization."

"Well, Father, you are home now. Here is your home. Do not look back. I am deeply sorry that all this mess is happening. However, we can all learn from and celebrate the innocence and hope in our new baby's life."

"Ah, Son, this is good," Serkan stated simply. The two men hugged each other warmly.

"Yes. We will have no more talk of the evil in this world. Let us focus on this glorious day. Life begins anew, and so shall we all. I am so glad that I have returned in time to celebrate with you."

"And to celebrate with you, Father. You are now a grandfather. Please, come meet your grandson, Adlee Berat Raffi."

For Emine, isolation was the order of the first week following childbirth. The midwife stayed with the Raffi family for 6 days after the birth. Halime was ever-present to help also. And, though not traditional, Aydin paid particular attention. Upon the eventual departure of the midwife, he not only paid her in coins, but he added a couple of special gifts.

She tried to refuse his generosity, but the grateful man was insistent. She had known of his painful previous loss of both his wife and baby during a difficult childbirth. She could not refuse his gifts of gratitude. The midwife had done her very best to care for both Emine and little Adlee in this first week.

In truth, Emine and the baby received extra special treatment for a full 40 days. They were never once left alone, as these were considered the most vulnerable days needed for physical and spiritual healing and well-being.

"Thank you, Aydin," Emine began one afternoon when the couple was alone with Adlee. "You have been as loving with Adlee and me as if you had married me in a traditional manner and we had planned to have this baby. I thank you from the bottom of my heart."

"We did plan to have this baby." Aydin's comment confused Emine.

He continued. "When I committed to you, we made our plan. It may not have been traditional, but it was *our* plan... our commitment to each other and to our then unborn child. And, I hope, to our unborn children. Emine, I am not only here as your husband and father to Adlee. As we move forward, I hope you will honor me as your husband and father to more children."

Emine smiled. "I must confess that I had not thought that far ahead. Aydin, please remember that in my culture, my father may well have arranged for me to marry someone I had not ever seen before the wedding week. In time, it is expected that we would grow to love each other.

"But with you, Aydin, I have a husband who was already a family friend since we were children... when I must confess, I had a bit of a crush on you. Years passed. Times changed. Then you and your family took me in when I was most unceremoniously left alone.

"You have been more than considerate and caring. You are a very easy man to love. Of course, I hope we will have more children... together."

Aydin gave her a loving hug. "At the end of your isolation, our tradition is to not only welcome you and our baby. But especially in royalty and ranking circles of society, there will be a special day of great celebration. You are my princess, my royalty. Because I am blessed with the financial means, this shall include dancing and great feasting. And the revelry is apt to go long into the night!"

"Oh, my goodness!" Emine was genuinely surprised. "I had no idea."

"Well, these celebrations are not typical throughout society. However, I have attained a certain... social status, thanks to my successful business dealings. We will have a splendid celebration.

"In truth, my beloved wife, I have been thinking about this and quietly planning for a couple of weeks now. There will be many decorations, torch lights in our courtyard, and several musicians. Mother has been working on a menu. And she is including items she recalls your mother serving, too.

"Emine, I am mindful of the fact that you did not get to enjoy a traditional wedding celebration. And I know what an amazing event that would have been. I have never forgotten the incredible wedding reception that your family hosted a few years ago at your summer home by Lake Van."

Now Aydin had her attention. Emine quipped, "Oh, Aydin! I had forgotten that Aram invited you!"

"Well, I remember clearly. It was most impressive *and* unforgettable. In some small way, I hope to let this celebration of our baby secretly double as a sort of reception for our wedding. It will not be in that beautiful setting, nor include as many people, but I will do everything I can to make this celebration as festive and wonderful as the one that your parents hosted following your sister's wedding on Akhtamar Island."

A Present-Day Reaction
19

"WHAT!!??! WHAT SISTER'S wedding on Akhtamar Island?" Cassie sat shocked. Had she heard incorrectly? She remembered her Grampa Hrant Gulumian talking about the details of a wedding in the great Cathedral of the Holy Cross back when he was a very young boy. He also had distinctly remembered the torchlight, music, dancing, and many lavish foods served at the reception that had followed at their summer home on Lake Van.

"Nane, of course." Nuray appeared confused. She looked at her mother and then back at Cassie before continuing. "How did you not know who got married at that wedding?"

"I don't know," replied a bewildered Cassie. "Grampa Hrant shared many detailed remembrances of the wedding and reception. He was a very little boy, barely more than a toddler, so I guess he never made the connection between the wedding and his own family. But as he grew older, I would think he should have known. Did she move far away?"

Nuray nodded. "Yes, as was customary, she moved to be with her husband's family here in Constantinople. But before we talk about that, perhaps we should see if you know of all the other children."

"Well, let's see... Historically, I know that my great-grandparents were born in 1870 and 1871. Garabed

Ohannes Gulumian was born in Van, Armenia. And Aghavni Gadera Samargian was born in Salmast, Armenia, near the Persian border... in modern day Iran.

"Their first son was Ohannes Garabed Gulumian, born in 1888. He became known as John in America. Oh, and Sidika, I met your Uncle Ohannes when I was just a child."

Sidika smiled. "Ah, Miss Cassie, I am so glad to know that. Please continue."

"Well, I do not recall too much about him. I know that I was 10 years old when he died in the state of New Hampshire, where I was raised.

"Then there was their second son, Aram, who was born in 1893. He also immigrated to the United States to attend a university. I remember him well on their family farm in Salisbury, NH. I also know... or at least I believe... that 4-½ years after Aram was born, Vahram and his twin sister Nazeli were born. Nazeli, who became Emine... your mother. Then in 1901, Anush, the youngest sister was born. That was followed by their youngest child and my future grandfather, Hrant on March 6, 1906."

The room grew still for more than just a moment. Nuray then looked at her mother and back to Cassie before speaking again.

"All that sounds accurate. But... you did not know that an elder daughter was born to Garabed and

Aghavni in 1890, two years after Ohannes. And she was named Nane."

"Such a beautiful name," thought Cassie aloud. "Please, tell me about her."

Nuray smiled and looked at her mother. Sidika nodded and began to speak.

"My Aunt Nane was a most beautiful woman. Her name means Armenian goddess, and she lived up to her name." Sidika continued, "The wedding that her baby brother recalled was her wedding to Armen Petrosyan, may he rest in peace. Please, Nuray, share the information from my mother's letters about Nane."

Nuray reached for a fresh pile of note paper. Before starting to read, however, she looked back up at Cassie with concern on her face.

"Cassie, Great Aunt Nane's story is a very complicated one. You already know about the... 'difficult' times the Armenians had due to the Ottoman's insecurities and distrust. But you may not have great awareness of another frustratingly evil part of our history. This was far from a 'peaceful ethnic cleansing' as many would still prefer the world to believe.

"The Ottomans were killing males and dehumanizing women. Believe me when I tell you that the Ottomans could not have cared less about simply moving Armenians to areas where they would be more comfortable."

Nodding, Cassie spoke. "Sure... moving them to places where they would be more comfortable... like deserts, graves and harems."

"Sadly," Sidika now added. "Those stories are far from 'tall tales.' I realize there are Turks today who try to claim that such activities never took place. Some even call the reports outrageous folklore. However, the truth is that the Ottomans felt a powerful need to take very large concentrations of Armenians and destroy them... one way or another.

"The Turks despised the Armenians not only for their Christian religion. They also distrusted the Armenians' passion for knowledge and education, not to mention their highly enlightened reverence for women. The leaders did not consider Armenians to even be worthy, unless, of course, you are talking about finding women to mother their children. Then they wanted the Armenians."

Nuray added, "Please understand that the Ottoman culture was inconsistent when it came to women. Peasant women were expected to labor in the fields, but if your family had any level of status... well, let's just say that mobility and visibility outside the home could become extremely constrained. Also, what we now view as disrespectful and unequal treatment today was not just levied on Christian women. Muslim women could also struggle for respect, and they were considered most fortunate if they ended up married to a man who practiced the protective teachings of Islam with sincere benevolence."

Now Sidika tsk-tsked out loud before she spoke. "I always believed that such thinking came from male logic. The Ottoman leadership seemed to actually fear women. This fear ran so deeply that 'protection' often meant 'isolation'... as if a woman would be easily led astray if given the opportunity. One popular philosophy literally held that an immoral women led to an immoral society."

"Hmmm... what about immoral men?" Nuray shrugged as she posed the question. She then looked down at the pages she held that shared the challengingly painful story. "Well, shall we start in happier times... following Nane's wedding?"

"Yes, please," implored Cassie. She knew she may now have even more ancestors to track.

"Garabed Gulumian had met the Petrosyan family years earlier during his travels to Istanbul... then still officially Constantinople. The marriage between Armen and Nane was arranged not long after that. Following the wedding, Nane left with Armen and other members of the Petrosyan family to return to Constantinople.

Initially, many letters were exchanged, but times became challenging, so letters became few and far between. When the troubles began, all contact was lost. They never reconnected. The last the family knew, Nane had just given birth to their second daughter."

"Oh!" Cassie remarked. "They had two children!"

"No," Nuray continued. "Mama later learned that they had three. The first-born was a daughter, followed by a son and a second daughter."

Cassie smiled. "Oh, my! How lovely!"

"Well, I am sorry to say that their story has its own deep sadness and share of heartbreak."

Cassie felt in no way deterred. "This means that you know their story!"

"Oh, yes. Mother got it all written down directly from Emine's words." Sidika nodded, which encouraged Cassie.

"So, Nazeli... I mean Emine was able to find her sister, even with the raging war? Please, tell me, how did she find her?"

Nuray took a deep breath before continuing. "Well, let me start with a little background, because the times were intriguing to say the least. I think all possible tears had been shed. The Great War had ended. There was a tremendous amount of misery and poverty. And illness. Don't forget about the Spanish Flu.

"Indeed, thousands of lives, both Christian and Muslim, had been lost to famine and illness that had nothing to do with war... and nothing to do with Ottoman atrocities against the Christians or any Armenian defensive attempts or reprisals.

"Please know, Cassie, that we are among the growing number of Turks who *do* know that the Ottomans did indeed carry out a planned elimination of Armenians... and any Muslims who sympathized or aided Christians. The parades of Armenians toward the deserts of Syria were death marches, not peaceful deportations.

"I know perfectly well that there are a great many Turks, including most government officials, who still live by what you Americans call 'the party line.' They practice and preach what they have been repeatedly taught since what we now call World War I ended. However, denials do not change the facts of history."

Now Cassie interjected. "I know what you are saying. One Turkish acquaintance of mine in America was insistent that the Ottomans were... in his words... 'merely relocating a minority population to places where they would be more comfortable.' So, genocide was committed for Armenian safety and comfort?"

Cassie shook her head as she continued. "My stomach knotted tightly, and I felt sick listening to him. We had to agree to disagree. Oh, but not him. He scoffed most arrogantly at me and made his ongoing disgust with... and continuing hatred of Armenians very clear."

Nuray reached forward and gently held Cassie's hand before speaking. "I am very sorry for that. Most Turks only know what they have been officially taught for generations now. We are all sadly indoctrinated repeatedly to believe, without a doubt, that the so-called rare incidences of violence against the Armenians were purely to prevent an expected revolution. Or perhaps they occurred to stop violence against Muslim civilians by Armenian gangs of raiders. Or they might have happened in mere defensive activities.

"The relocation exercises were for show at best. Most of the women, children, and elderly in those marches were slaughtered outright. The few groups that made it as far as Aleppo had lost most of the civilians due to dehydration, starvation, exposure, or outright violence along the road.

"Oh, and who truly knows how high the numbers of Armenians massacred really goes? No one seems to mention this, but I remember that in Ottoman Empire times, they did not even keep records of female births. Women were not included in population figures. I believe any numbers reported by anyone only reflect male lives lost.

"Regardless of how many Armenians the Ottomans slaughtered, it would not help their Empire survive. In fact, I think the Ottomans taught a peace-loving people to stand up for themselves, to stop believing the empty Ottoman promises, and to even fight back."

"Agreed," was Cassie's initial response. "But I fear that the distrust between Turks and Armenians remains strong, at least partially because of the ongoing official denials."

Sidika, though weary, spoke firmly now. "As my mother used to say, 'One should not feel hurt at the kick of an ass.' But it would be impossible for Armenians to not feel crushed. Ongoing denial is useless. I would call it a cover-up."

"Oh, Mama, it's not as if they were the first regime to do something unsavory. We may as well call it politics as usual. Historians agree and the war crimes trials showed that the Ottoman leadership used the ongoing disturbances caused by war as shields, while they carried out their... obnoxious acts against Christians."

"Nuray... Sidika... we in the United States certainly have our own 'denial' issues." Cassie continued. "Some people truly think they can rewrite history or somehow erase details that modern thinkers now view as heinous. But rewording history books, changing street names and holidays, and tearing down statues of earlier leaders is, in my opinion, filled with folly.

"For example, if we are honest with ourselves and do just a bit of research, we will recognize that most early trade ships carried slaves, most new people in our original colonies arrived as various sorts of indentured servants, and yes... we even had Presidents who 'owned' slaves.

"For me, it's all proof positive that we humans are very slow to evolve. But stomping on the names of past leaders does not alter or correct society's past actions. As ugly as some facts may be, they are part of our history and should be taught precisely as that. We need not be proud of every facet of our history.

"Denial of ill deeds doesn't right any wrongs. I think we do better when we recognize and denounce our past issues, rather than trying to minimize them or make retributions. I also believe in the sage remarks that we must remember our history, or we are destined to repeat it."

Sidika offered the first reply to Cassie. "We Brits can sometimes think of Americans as isolated and unaware. But Cassie, I am impressed by your awareness and the wisdom you have acquired. Denials often help societies or population segments rationalize that they can do whatever they want to people and get away with it. The facts and evidence can merely be destroyed or even rewritten. What they do not understand is that denials, destruction, and rewrites will never change history."

Cassie rose, crossed to Sidika, and gave the elderly woman a tender hug. "I agree. History will stand. The truth will come out, or as the Armenian proverb says, 'The feet of a lie are short.' I wish individuals and societies could learn to simply accept, apologize, and move on... but behave better in doing so!"

"Even in your young nation, the lack of such awareness raises eyebrows here," Nuray added. "Also in other societies, I know. You Americans have groups that think millions of dollars paid by today's working taxpayers to descendants of the slavery era will somehow be fair retribution. Foolishness. Imagine if we were to pay retribution to all individuals who have suffered discrimination and horrors due to enslavement, civilian massacres, and eons of political power struggles! I doubt anyone alive would *not* be warranted retribution."

"Ah, Nuray, *your* wisdom is remarkable." Cassie continued. "If we all keep talking with each other, and communicating respectfully with each other, perhaps someday we *will* learn to be fair and kind and less judgmental. Someday."

"Well, it certainly isn't happening now any more than it was when the Ottoman Empire was collapsing. You are right when you observe that we humans are slow to evolve."

Nuray continued. "The Ottomans had said that they merely struggled with what to do with all the Muslim refugees who were flocking back to the area now known as Turkey. As they continued to lose Ottoman Empire territories throughout Europe and North Africa, the refugee numbers grew at an alarming rate. Somehow, they convinced themselves that removing Armenians would free up homes and villages for Turks. What that argument fails to take into account is the fact that they massacred far more Armenians than they relocated."

Now Sidika spoke again. "And they burned and destroyed entire villages. As you well know, they even obliterated what was the flourishing ancient city of Van. And I mean that they deliberately demolished every single home, every garden wall, every church, and even every tree. My grandfather Raffi wept as he spoke of this. The Ottomans left a crushed wasteland so the Armenians would have nothing to which to return anyway, even if they did survive.

"So, if a government is genuinely seeking more housing, none of this makes sense. Why destroy entire cities and villages? Not to mention their rounding up of Armenian scholars, leaders, and artisans, most of whom were then executed or imprisoned and tortured prior to execution."

The elderly woman's voice was soft, but steady. As a Turk herself, she deeply wished she could obliterate a few chapters of history from her own mind.

She continued. "I am still flabbergasted to think the Young Turks leaders could have felt so deeply threatened by Armenians, a population they regularly tried to denounce as dramatically inferior.

"So, they now have enacted laws to prevent the use of language that might denigrate their Turkishness. In Turkey, one mustn't speak of the 'genocide.' Oh, no. We must use delicate, less convicting words like 'calamity.' To speak otherwise might be seen as too insulting to the nation. But they did this. *We* did this. Our forefathers. They should openly accept it, sincerely apologize, and move forward. Instead, we have been now teaching generations of Turkish children the government's desired fairytales."

Cassie hoped to steer conversation back to family matters. "I recall many reports and even photographs of the scholar round up in Constantinople. It happened in April 1915. Was Nane, the eldest Gulumian sister in Constantinople at then?"

The server had now finished clearing their table at the Al Basha café. Sidika suggested that she was very weary, so the question would be best answered in the next folder the following day. However, she left Cassie with a haunting thought.

"We finally learned what happened to my grandmother Aghavni and the boys thanks to you publishing your grandmother's journal that included Hrant's story. However, you never knew that one of the two tortured sisters lived through their nightmare. And you never knew until now that there was also an elder sister."

Sidika's pace now slowed considerably. "Nuray will share from the next folder tomorrow. For now, just know that you likely saw your great uncle... the husband of that eldest sister... in one of the 1915 photographs... one showing the line ups of Armenian scholars, taken before they were imprisoned... or executed. Tomorrow you will learn more through the words of my mother."

Escapade in Escape
20

EMINE'S HEART WAS full. Her first-born, Adlee, was now six years old. He was smart and kind, just like Aydin, his papa. He was doting on a new baby sister. Sidika was not quite one year old.

Aydin was very pleased. His children were healthy. Their home had thus far survived the famines and flus. Fruits and vegetables flourished in the once flower-filled, walled garden. Emine's gardening and culinary skills proved to be even more valuable in their home than her craftsmanship with the needle and thread.

He wrapped his arm around his wife's waist. "You work wonders with everything you touch. I am grateful that my business continues to be able to provide many blessings for our family."

"I am also thankful for you and how hard you work to provide for us." Emine continued. "As my mother used to say, 'When God gives, He gives with both hands.' And yes, we are mightily blessed."

Aydin smiled. He always liked hearing Emine repeat pleasant Armenian proverbs she recalled from her youth. "I think He blessed me because you would be coming back into my life. And you deserve as many blessings as possible."

His cousin Yavuz had returned to them with a wife and toddler in tow. Aydin and Emine were grateful to be able to take the trio in during this time of great post-war need. Yavuz now had his own story of rescue and renewed tolerance. Following a dastardly raid on an Armenian village, he had found Luseres, who soon became his bride. Later they had learned that the Great War had already ended, but his regiment had not yet received word.

"Even years later, it still grieves my heart deeply to have been part of this regiment," sighed Yavuz. "Our captain ordered us to enter village after village. We were sent house by house to find any Armenians who may be hiding. The captain then ordered them to line up on the main street... the elderly, the women, and down to the tiniest baby. With total disregard, each person was then beheaded. Those who tried to escape were shot in the back, and then their bodies... well, there is no polite way to say it."

"In the name of Allah!" Ayden proclaimed. "How did Luseres escape?"

"Ah! She had been staying at a neighbor's home, where the mother had just borne a new baby son. As the assistant to the midwife, Luseres stayed on to care for the new mother and baby. However, in the middle of the night, the father started waking everyone in the household. With great urgency, he told them all that they must leave the village immediately before the sun could rise."

Yavuz continued. "He said that he had a premonition. An angel had appeared to him and issued a grave warning that something was going to happen the next day, so they had better pack up all the belongings they could carry on the donkeys and prepare to leave as quickly as possible. His wife thought it was very poor judgment for her to be riding on a bouncy donkey so soon after having given birth, but she did not argue with him. Luseres promised to accompany her for the first hours, just to be sure. So, the little family left.

"By noon the next day, the wife assured Luseres that she was fine, and advised her to turn back to rejoin her own family in the village. You cannot imagine the horrors she saw. Everyone had been lined up and massacred. They were all dead. Her family, her neighbors, her friends. Everyone. Gone. Her village was now a walled shell filled with death.

"She had no time to grieve or even think of what to do next. She suddenly heard the sound of horse hooves clip-clopping down the street toward her. Luseres dashed behind the well to hide, shaking with grief, anger, and fear. Little did she know that she had nothing to fear from me."

Yavuz sadly smiled at his young bride as he reached over and took her hand. "My captain had sent me back to do a final check on the village... to be sure that no one had survived. Too many stories had surfaced about a village being eliminated, but one or two people somehow survived to tell the truth of the nightmare that had taken place.

"Of course, I found the terrified young woman immediately. I consoled her the best I could, gave her water, and promised her safety. Naturally, I took her away from that place to hide her, assuring her that I would return to help her. When I got back to my regiment, I learned the war was over, and we were all told to go home. Gathering Luseres, I realized that my home no longer existed either. My village just south of the walled city of Van had been obliterated by the Ottomans because so many Armenians had lived there. The government promised to eventually rebuild, but that did not solve our immediate housing issue."

"Cousin, why did you not come straight back to me then, rather than now... years later?" Aydin was dumbfounded.

"In truth, I was somewhat overwhelmed. It was shocking to see block after block of rubble where the ancient city of Van had once stood for so many centuries. After the Russians had left, and we took the city back from the Armenians, I had seen the incredible damage from the battles, yes. And I knew about the orders to then destroy the city. But unexpectedly, in my own time of homelessness, the full weight of the utter destruction hit me.

"I just wanted to leave the area... quickly. I had heard of some housing for troops and their families in Bitlis, so we headed there. I knew I could force Luseres to convert to Islam, and I told her it was Allah's will for her to do so. Whether she believed me or not, I will not likely ever know. I am fully aware that she felt obligated to me, and she agreed to convert and marry me. I guess marrying a homeless wretch like me seemed more appealing than risking deportation or worse."

"Yavuz, please tell me that you would not have turned her in to the authorities." Aydin's tone showed he was unsure. "Would you?"

"No, no no. That did not even cross my mind!" Yavuz now beamed broadly. "But she did not know that."

Aydin rolled his eyes. But Yavuz now looked at his bride and smiled. "It felt very nice to be needed. And now we have a child." Luseres smiled back and demurely cast her eyes downward.

Aydin wanted to learn more. "So, tell me... what changed that caused you to leave Bitlis?"

"Ahhhh. We learned of the U.S. President's plan to return the four largest provinces of Anatolia back to the Armenians... the ones that had been home to a majority population of Armenians."

"But, Cousin, we all know that Armenians barely exist throughout just a few pockets of Anatolia by now. They certainly do not constitute a majority population any longer."

"True. However, we knew many Armenians had escaped to Russia. And many had settled in Yerevan in the province further to the east. Turkish Muslim refugees from Europe and North Africa were being resettled into the four formerly Armenian provinces. But quite frankly, we were fearful of any potential retaliation by the Armenians who might try to come back home. They had lost everything.

"Though the Treaty of Sèvres requires our leadership to return all acquired property, homes, lands, and wealth back to Armenians, I cannot see how this is to be possible. It's gone. The money was spent on the war... or pocketed by those in high-ranking positions. Goods have vanished. IOUs are meaningless. Everything is gone."

"Along with the Armenians," Aydin wryly added.

"Exactly! So, how can we Turks return what we don't have to people who are... well, no longer here?"

"Remember Cousin, we have new leadership. The Ottomans lost when Germany lost. We are now part of a new Republic that is still forming. New boundaries ceded back to Armenia most of the Armenian provinces, including Erzzurum, Trabzon, Van, and Bitlis, with no Turkish military forces allowed to be anywhere near the Armenian borders. Well, that did not go over well here at home. Our new Turkish Republic leaders easily took advantage of the fact that the Allied Powers were busy rebuilding their own nations. They also repudiated the results of losing the Great War as if it had been lost by someone other than the Turks, so they decided the new Republic of Turkey did not have to comply. Everything will work out now. You are safe with us here."

"And we thank you, Aydin," Yavuz said sincerely. "I thought Constantinople... now Istanbul would be safer in these changing times, but I was not sure whether or not I would still be welcomed."

"Foolishness," came Aydin's reply. "You are family. My family. You have followed orders and done things you wish you had not done. We will pray to Allah on these things today. Had you not followed orders, remember, you would have landed in deep trouble as a sympathizer. These are still very problematic times."

"I thank you. We thank you. And you are right about the times. We must now do something about all the poverty, the famines, and the illness. Aydin, we will count on you to guide us as to how we can help with these issues."

"Emine has extensive experience in this area. Through her mother, she was active in collecting items for refugees during the start of the Great War. Now she is even more valuable. The missionaries have started some very large orphanages. These are now sites for schools and homeless women, too. Most of the refugees are women and children.

"As you may recall, Emine is fluent in Turkish, Armenian, Kurdish, and French languages, as well as some English. The orphanages and clinics are desperate for translators. She and Mother have become regulars. The new baby is old enough, so Emine is going back today for the first time in months. We go there now, but we will be back before dinner. Come observe if you like. Today will be special. Some new volunteers are arriving to teach music and dancing."

"Aydin, I think we will let you go along without us. You can tell us about it later. I would like Luseres to have a little more time for adjustment to the new household before any new outside social activity."

Both Serkan and Ayden accompanied Halime and Emine on this day. Adlee and baby Sidika were with them. The atmosphere at the orphanage was unusually festive. With baby Sidika on her hip, Emine and her mother-in-law went about their duties. They folded laundry, mended clothing, and tended to the homeless women, with Emine serving as a translator between the Armenian refugees and the Turkish volunteers.

Adlee was content to stay with his father and grandfather, especially on this day. The dancing looked fun. He quickly joined the boys' group and was soon dancing along with the others.

A brilliantly raucous laugh suddenly lilted across the yard. Emine stood straight up. Memories flashed through her mind, and she couldn't breathe.

Whirling about, Emine moved a few steps toward the dancers. A man standing just in front of her turned to face the little lad he was instructing, who happened to be her own little Adlee. She saw the man's face, and her jaw dropped.

"Toros! Toros Kherbekian?" Emine immediately slapped her right hand over her mouth. Though inappropriate in Muslim culture to initiate such a conversation, she had not been able to stop herself.

The man immediately did a doubletake at her. Toros froze as if he had just seen a ghost.

The Reunion

21

"NAZELI?" TOROS SPOKE at barely a whisper. "I... I thought you were..."

"I was. Or I thought I was. Everyone thought I was. We thought you were gone also. A family friend found me still alive. He and his wife took me in and nursed me back to health. I have not converted, but I live in a Muslim household, and I am married to their son."

"You look wonderful. I am so very glad you are alive and well." Toros smiled and looked at the baby on her hip. "And this little one. She is yours?"

"Yes, this is my youngest. Sidika is her name."

Aydin had observed the exchange between Emine and the dance instructor. He now approached them with concern.

"Excuse me, is there a problem?" Aydin's brow furrowed.

"No, no, my dear. We have all just had a very big surprise. Aydin, my husband... this is Toros, the one we thought had been killed."

"Ahhh, you mean your former fiancé. I think I recall you from our youth. I was a friend of her brother Aram." Aydin looked at Toros. "Emine told me of your loss and the loss of her remaining family."

"Ah, yes. I thought I was dead, too. But it is nice to see you again," Toros said, before turning to her. "Emine? Is that your name now?"

"Yes, Toros. For my protection during the bad times, my name was changed to Emine, though I certainly did not feel at all courageous, nor fearless, as the name suggests."

Toros continued. "And you said this baby is your youngest. You have other children?"

Aydin answered now. "Yes, Toros. Our son Adlee is the boy you were just instructing."

"Well!" Toros said, flashing his legendary smile. "It is very nice to meet you, Adlee. Young man, you were just dancing with my own son. Tavit, say hello to Adlee."

The two lads stood next to each other. They turned to each other, smiled broadly, and shook hands.

Toros looked again at Emine. She briefly met his gaze and then, appropriately for the culture and times, cast her eyes downward.

Aydin continued. "My father had received word that everyone in your regiment... had been..."

"Ah yes, the Ottomans disarmed us, lined us up, and shot us all. Yes, you can speak it out loud. Two of us survived their ghastly executions, however. I ended up in an underground cave system near Van, recovering from my gunshot wounds. Fortunately for me, I was nursed back to health by the young woman who is responsible for saving Nazeli's... I mean Emine's mother, and her twin and baby brothers."

"What?!? They escaped?" Emine's jaw dropped, and she now looked up, directly at Toros.

"Yes! Before leaving the walled city, they ran from the line of Armenians being deported. Arexi saw them and hid them. Then she and her brother, Tavit helped them escape. Arexi and Tavit then found me in the caves. We named our son after her brother. We lost him in the final battle at Van. Nazeli... Emine, it was your mother who told me that you had been killed. But, I am sorry, we were not able to learn the fates of your mother and brothers after they were secreted out of the underground and headed on their way to Kars."

By this point, Serkan and Halime had joined the group and were listening intently. Arexi was also standing beside Toros.

Serkan spoke. "I am the family friend and former Ottoman soldier who found that Emine... Nazeli... was still alive. Aydin, her husband, is my son."

"My deepest respect and thanks to you both," Toros said acknowledging the two men. "Nazeli has remained precious in my heart and mind. Such a twist of fate that we should all meet this way now. I believed she was dead, but she lives. She thought I was dead, but I live. I live much in thanks to Arexi, now my wife." He put his arm around Arexi's shoulders.

Just then, a woman's soft voice could be heard. She hesitantly called out from a darkened corner behind them.

"Nazeli? Nazeli Gulumian? Is that really you, sister?"

Lost Is Found

22

EMINE WHIRLED AROUND. A woman sat huddled alone on the floor in the corner. How had she not previously seen the figure fully draped in shawls?

"Excuse me?" Emine approached the woman and crouched down beside her. "How do you know me by that name? And the Gulumian name?"

Ever so gently she then reached toward the woman and lifted a trembling chin ever so slightly. As the light from the room crossed her face, Emine choked back a gasp. The heavily tattooed features could not disguise the beauty of her eldest sister.

"Nane! My darling!"

"Do not look at me, sister," implored Nane. "I am ashamed."

"Nonsense!" Emine's shock was masked by her vocal tone, which was firm but compassionate. "You are forever my beloved sister."

Emine had already seen many Armenian and Greek women with faces heavily tattooed by tyrants who had bought and kept them as sex slaves. The markings indicated the man's complete power over the woman and promised to keep her banished from ever fitting in with her own people again, never mind being accepted by another man.

With tears streaming down the faces of both women, Emine proceeded to kiss each and every irregular ink blot on her sister's forehead, cheeks, and chin. "I love you. I love you. I love you." She repeated her words with each tender kiss.

The Raffis, Toros, and all the children had gathered around the two women at this point. The two re-united sisters seemed utterly oblivious.

"You are safe now. Where is Armen? Your children?"

Nane shook her head. "My husband is gone. Our home is gone. I have been looking for my children in every orphanage for two years now. All... is lost."

"You are not lost. You, my dear sister, are found."

Emine looked up at Aydin imploringly. Her husband had already read the scenario perfectly. He nodded his head and gestured for Emine to bring her sister.

"Please, Nane," began Emine as she and Aydin helped Nane up from the floor. "Please meet my husband Aydin and our children Adlee and Sidika. And my father- and mother-in-law. You may well remember them as family friends from Van, Serkan and Halime Raffi. Also, my dear friend Toros and his wife Arexi and son Tavit."

Cordialities were shared. Then final farewell formalities were exchanged between Toros and Emine.

The Raffis then returned home. Emine and Halime kept their arms wrapped around Nane. Aydin carried Sidika, and Serkan accompanied them, hand-in-hand with little Adlee.

Arriving home, Nane did not want to rest. She felt energized after finding her sister. They shared some food and put the children to bed. The adults then retired to the walled garden to talk. They sat in a pleasant grouping of benches and chairs beside the grape arbor.

Aydin opened the conversation. "Are you certain you wish to do this? I mean, with all of us here. If you prefer, we can all leave you and Emine in private."

"In truth, there has been enough misunderstanding, pain, and loss over these past few years to fill many lifetimes." Nane continued, "I believe you all should know what has happened and is still happening."

Emine reached forward and placed her hand upon her sister's hand. Then she spoke.

"Nane, please share with us whatever you wish. I trust this family around us just as we trusted our own family back in Van. Yes, they are Turkish and Muslim, but they were good friends of our Papa's, and they saved my life. You can have confidence and trust in them. They are also kind and loving. Plus, they have full awareness that the Ottoman leadership planned, sanctioned, and carried out some very wicked activities against the Christians, especially against us Armenians."

"I understand," replied Nane. "And I thank you for your hospitality. I have not slept in a real home in so long and have grown rather accustomed to streets and shelters."

Emine shook her head. "Those days are behind you. You can ask anything of us. Remember what Papa used to say. 'He that asks knows one shame; he that doesn't knows two.' Oh, how I wish we had found you sooner! Please, Nane, would you not prefer to get some rest before opening all these deep, emotional wounds?"

"No, dear sister," Nane said softly. "As Mama used to say, 'The world agrees in one word. Time is golden.' And I grow increasingly unwell. I do not know how much time we truly have, and there is no time to spare. I have found you, and now you must know. You all should know."

"Of course, Nane," Emine replied gently. "Please tell us what has happened."

"I want to start with the... unexpected evening that ultimately tore my family apart back in April 1915. It has been seven years since this all happened, but sometimes it feels as if it was just yesterday. My husband, Arman Petrosyan, was dining with a couple of associates at a popular restaurant. He had known these two merchant friends, Krikor Onnikian and Kevork Terjumanian, for many years.

"Suddenly, police burst in and started arresting men left and right. They took everyone! I knew something was terribly wrong when he failed to come home. And word spread quickly through the city. I soon learned he was among many dozens of men who had been arrested.

"There seemed to be no good cause. They were not rebellious, not military. Most had little in common. The Ottomans had arrested publishers and politicians, book sellers and money changers, composers and novelists, butchers and professors, lawyers and scientists, tailors and pharmacists, architects, and craftsmen. I know that a few were members of the Armenian National Assembly, and I am sure that some political activists were among the groups, but it seemed the Ottomans were simply sweeping the streets of Armenian intellectuals and leaders in all walks of life.

"I learned of some people who had gone to the jails and holding cells to try and find their loved ones and perhaps earn their release. But they ended up getting arrested too!"

Aydin now commented. "You are quite right, Nane. Tehcir Law had officially been enacted. These were special measures to enable the police and military forces to deport all Armenians. What happened, however, was widespread elimination. We are so very sorry. Please... continue with your story."

"I did not know what to do. For the next day I sat... numb... just waiting with the children. A few neighbors came by in the morning. The news they brought was confusing, at best, and terrifying, at worst."

Arrest of Intellectuals
23

"THEY TOLD ME that the officials had been lining the men up and taking group photographs on the city streets. Some were then transferred to some faraway prisons. Some were hanged right along the streets of Constantinople. I will never forget my little Arevig's mournful plea. 'Where's Papa? When will he be home?' I did not know how to answer her. But I didn't have long to wait. By nightfall, our door opened, and in he walked!"

"Such a blessing!" Emine then asked, "Did he know why he had been released?"

"Hah! He didn't even have a clear idea as to why he'd been arrested in the first place. Or his friends for that matter. And his two friends were *not* released. And none of them were conspirators against the Ottomans. They had not committed any offense.

"Well, needless to say, we hugged. We wept. We talked, and we even managed to laugh a bit. He was ravenous, as the jailors had fed the men nothing. So, we gathered the family around, and we ate."

"But Nane, why was Armen released and not the others?" Emine posed just one of the many questions everyone was thinking.

"Some of the other men were also released. There were no explanations. The only thing that the officers would say to my Armen was that he had been in the wrong place at the wrong time."

"Then this was good news!" Emine smiled at Nane.

"We thought so, yes. And yet, we were very concerned for our friends. For all our people. If the Ottomans could randomly imprison leaders, what hope remained for the rest of us? And sadly, tragically, we learned that several of those arrested with my sweet Armen had already been executed. There would be no conversations... no honest charges... no appealing to reason... and no chance for a trial."

Serkan now spoke up. "So much for the Ottomans' promise of fairness for Armenians. As a former soldier, I sadly witnessed many such... inconsistencies. They all ended badly for the Armenians. I apologize for my people... for our former Young Turks leadership, which was disingenuous at best. This must have been terrifying for you all."

"Oh, yes, sir... it was. The military presence was everywhere. Armenian weapons had already been confiscated by the Ottomans much earlier. We were left at the mercy of a merciless government.

"So, I admit that we slept very little that night. The children slept soundly, because they could not fathom the seriousness of the crisis. In the morning, however, all hope of sanity vanished."

Nane wept again. She just shook her head.

"Oh, dear sister," exclaimed Emine. "Perhaps we have talked enough for now. You need rest."

"No," came Nane's immediate and frantic rebuttal. "There will be plenty of time for rest... later... too soon perhaps. I must tell you everything... now. The Ottomans were not what they seemed!"

"I know. We know." Emine looked at the little group listening intently. "You are safe now. Please try to be calm."

"You are right, Nazeli... I mean Emine." Then Nane spat on the ground by the garden bench on which she sat, as if that would help her cast the taste of disgusting memories from her mind. Then she continued.

"My sincere apologies to you all. When my sister tells me that you are kind and open-minded and understanding, I know I can trust her. And I want to believe. But even this family made my sister change her name to something Turkish."

Emine spoke right up. "That was for my protection, Nane. Remember, the Raffi family saved my life back in our home city of Van. If they'd slipped and used my given name in the wrong circles, it could have meant torture and death for us all. Please, dear sister, continue telling us what happened to you back in that fateful April of 1915."

"Well, it was just a day later. Armen was not going to work. The city felt eerie and unsafe. Very few people dared to be seen on the streets. They were hanging some leading Armenians... right in public. And they were pronouncing them to be criminals without even offering legitimate charges. Anyone even close to the holding cells could hear the painful wails of men being tortured inside. We simply hid at home. But that was not enough to save us.

"When Armen answered the next knock on the door, we thought it was a fellow Armenian bringing more information or else needing shelter. Wrong. As soon as he opened the door, the officer standing there shot him. Shot him dead in our doorway where he stood. I cried out and swept our children into my arms.

"There was nothing we could do. The men took us all outside and away from our home in mere seconds. Because we had learned the Turkish language as children, I understood all that they were saying.

"The children would be placed in an orphanage, and I was to be... sold... sold as a slave to some aristocrat who was close to the sultan. There was nothing fancy about the proceedings. I was thrown like a bag of grain into a small, dank room. Guards stood at the door and outside the window.

"The other Armenian women in the room were whimpering. They'd also lost husbands and children. What was to become of us, indeed! They could not help but believe that we would all likely be ravaged and then murdered, but I had understood the men's words. I knew what lurked ahead for us.

"We were in a holding cell. We might avoid the deadly fate the other women feared... in trade for another undesirable one. If one of the sultan's men or a high commander found any of us to be suitable, they would pay for us to become slaves in the household harem. That could mean kitchen work or other domestic duties. We might even be ordered to care for children. Or... we might become sex slaves.

"I tried to whisper this information to the other women. I told them to not lose heart. We prayed."

"Then a royal guard entered and ordered us to stop speaking. The officers paraded us into a larger room. Three men were seated along a side wall amidst large, colorful pillows and cushions. They sat there drinking coffee, chatting, and laughing.

"Guards then offered the men a better view of... er... the merchandise being offered. They unceremoniously stripped off our clothing, dropping it at our feet."

Sold

24

EMINE AND HALIME sat listening to Nane's tale in shock. They were glad that the children had been put to bed and were not able to hear all this. Nane continued speaking, as if she had emotionally gone numb. She slowly began to unravel her sordid story.

"The two men seated on the side looked to the one in the center. It became obvious that he had the higher ranking and could choose first. His eyes locked on mine, which I am certain glowed with angry fire. I immediately looked down. Then a guard grabbed my arm and thrust me onto the floor at the man's feet.

"The burly man in his fancy robes gruffly put his hand under my chin. He lifted my quivering chin to force me to look at him. An evil grin slowly slid across his fat face. He released my chin and nodded to the guard."

"This one will do," he began. "And I will take the short one that was standing beside her, too."

"The guard pulled me up from the floor. Another guard grabbed the other woman's arm and our clothing. As we were pulled from the room, I reached out and grabbed her hand. There was a feigned sense of security in our togetherness... our shared tumultuous situation.

"The reality of our imprisonment soon became clear. We were delivered to a door in a small complex of buildings, all within an outer wall. A woman of about 60 years seemed very much in charge here. We soon learned that she was the aristocrat commander's mother. She took charge of all the women slaves and all the other females in the harem, including the commander's wives and their children.

"The Mother-Woman gestured to a couple of black servants, we later learned were eunuchs, sold as slaves in Africa. But the Ottomans had removed their male parts, because only eunuchs could serve as guards in the women's quarters. These eunuchs took us to a large room where several women were seated. I quickly realized that these people did not have to go to the public bath houses. This room served as a private bathing area for all the women in the house.

"Two of the women in the room, scantily draped in a creamy gauze fabric, approached us and began dutifully removing our clothing. I could not help but notice how routine, but gentle their approach was. How different from the guards at the... ahem... auction house.

"The bathing process was not only thorough, but also almost ceremonial. Everything smelled of violet petals. If not for the circumstances, I might have even called the process luxurious. However, I recognized that they were preparing us for something. Precisely what that was would become clear very soon. All I could think of during that process was the old Armenian proverb that says, 'Even if the nightingale is in a gold cage, she still dreams of returning to the forest.' Wrapping me up in fine fabrics and jeweled headpieces changed nothing. I was now a slave, plain and simple.

"The woman in charge re-appeared. In Turkish she started delivering instructions, which a young Armenian slave girl translated for us... until she realized I both understood and spoke Turkish also."

"She had declared, 'You will refer to me simply as Mother. There is to be no question of this. You will do whatever you are told to do here. This is your new home. From this day forward, you will not go outside this home, ever.'"

"What? You mean we can never walk in the sunshine again?" Nane had blurted out the words in Turkish without thinking. She immediately bit her tongue and looked down.

Nane remembered her many Turkish and French language lessons at home in Van, Armenia. Her father encouraged them by repeating the lesson, "You are as much of a person as the languages you know." But Nane had now revealed her education in a dangerous situation.

The Mother-Woman slowly walked to stand directly in front of Nane. She looked her up and down.

"Soooo, you understand and speak Turkish. This is true?"

Nane nodded and replied simply. "Yes."

"You will answer, 'Yes, Mother.'" The tone was almost threatening.

Nane's eyes now opened wide. She knew the woman was deadly serious.

"Yes, Mother."

"Good. This will please my son greatly. What other languages can you speak or read?"

"Kurdish. French. A little English." Nane was not sure how this was a good thing.

"Excellent. Do you know poetry, music, or dance?"

"Well, I have read poetry. As a child I learned to play music on a couple of instruments. And I learned several Armenian folk dances. Thank you for asking... Mother."

The woman nodded her head as she slowly walked around Nane, inspecting every bit of her skin, face and hair. She reached up and pulled away a couple of hair combs, causing Nane's hair to tumble loosely below her shoulders. The woman smiled broadly. She then turned to one of the eunuchs and made her announcement.

"This one is good. She is to be trained."

Looking back at Nane, she then posed a question. "And what was your given name?"

"My name is Nane, Mother." Nane was nervous.

"Your name *was* Nane. That will never do. And what is the meaning of that name?"

"I was my parents' first daughter. Nane means Armenian goddess."

The Mother-Woman chuckled. "Of course, it does. From now on, your name shall be... yes... Zehra. While not a goddess, this Turkish name reflects a beauty that blossoms and seems very fitting for you.

"Please... Mother... I mean no disrespect, but why must I get a new name? What is wrong with my own name, Nane?"

"Ah, you do not understand," Mother-Woman nodded her head before continuing. "You have been purchased by the household of Volkan Karakas. He is a dear friend and cousin of Sultan Mehmed V. Per the Sultan's wishes, you now serve at the will of Volkan."

"How should I address him?" Nane asked.

"No. You will not address him... ever. In fact, you will never look at him. Do not make eye contact at all. If he wishes anything... anything at all, he will tell you. And you will comply, always behaving in a sweet, pleasant manner. He may want you to read poetry or play music or dance. Or he may direct you to entertain his male guests. Or he may choose for you to bear him a child. But, whatever he asks, always remember that you are merely his property to do with as he wishes."

"Is he.... kind?" Nane was growing concerned.

Mother-Woman merely smiled a slight, but sad smile. "Too many questions," is all she then said.

Inked Out

25

SITTING IN THE harem's common room, Nane, now called Zehra, worked on some mending for her new master. At her side sat another Armenian concubine, named Ahu. But she could only speak Turkish.

"You are so young," Zehra remarked softly to Ahu. "You are beautiful and bright, but how is it that you know so much about the inner workings and... shall I say, politics of this household."

"I am not supposed to know of my Armenian background. According to our Mother-Woman, I am the daughter of Volcan and one of his wives, who... passed away a few years ago. Though forbidden to tell me, never mind teach about my heritage, my true mother was Armenian. Her family lived in Constantinople.

"Sadly, Ottoman soldiers and Kurds began killing Armenians in one province in 1894. The political pretense was to drive Armenians out, as we original local people were seen as second-class citizens. The massacres then spread to all Christians, but primarily Armenians and Assyrians. Leaders in Constantinople protested and sought reforms from Sultan Abdul Hamid, but massacres continued. When violence broke out in Constantinople itself in 1996, my mother was orphaned and sold to the father of Volkan Karakas. She lived the rest of her life here.

"So, am I to understand that he was your father?" Zehra was stunned.

"Of course. This is normal." Ahu continued. "They taught me Turkish and history. And I learned sewing, dancing, and poetry. Because I was born as a girl, my mother was not a favored concubine. But the good news was that I got to spend my childhood here in the harem where I could be close to her."

"Well, that was a blessing. I am sorry that you have not seen the outside world." Zehra continued. "There are many beautiful places outside these walls."

"I have been told that. However, such experiences are reserved for free citizens, not slaves."

"Ahu, does it trouble you to have been a slave all your life?"

"No. This is my place in life." That was all Ahu said.

"Perhaps you can tell me something. Do you know why some of the women here have been tattooed on their faces?"

"Oh, yes," came Ahu's quick reply. "This signifies that woman is the master's property. Do not fight it when they come to tattoo you, or it will only be worse for you. You can see from some of the other's faces that everyone is different, and some are very heavily marked."

"What!?! When they come for me?"

"Yes, they will. They always tattoo the new girls within a few days of arriving here."

"Then why... if you don't mind me asking... how is it that *you* have no tattoos?"

Ahu smiled. "Because the master was my father, I am no longer Armenian. I have Turkish blood."

Zehra's forehead scrunched. "I am sorry to not understand. If your mother was Armenian, aren't you also Armenian?"

"Oh, now I see your question." Ahu smiled. "The Ottomans have had many sultans during the past 600 years. Almost all of them did not have Turkish mothers. But it is only the father's blood that matters."

"Speaking of parents, it sounds as though your mother was very young."

"Oh, yes! I am 15, so I was born in 1900. She was just 15 herself."

Now Zehra became curious. "So, you said that your mother died young. I am very sorry you no longer have her with you."

"Yes, it was sad. But, because I was born a girl, the master did not want her any longer. But then he used her to entertain all his friends. She explained to me that she had become very sick from that. She felt numb all the time. Eventually, her legs were mostly paralyzed. And it was not long after that when she died."

Just then, two guards approached and ordered Zehra to put down her sewing and come with them. She looked at Ahu with concern.

"You will be fine," Ahu said. "Do not be afraid."

The guards took Zehra across the room and lifted her onto a table. One pushed her down on the table, and the other began to strap down her legs. Zehra began to flail her arms wildly.

"No! No!" Zehra protested to no avail. "What are you doing?"

The guard grabbed her arms and yelled at her gruffly. "Silence!"

The other guard who had tied her legs to the table now took one of her arms. Before tying it down, he stroked it gently, as if trying to calm her down.

"Please, girl," this guard said. "You will be marked now, but not further harmed. Try not to struggle, or it can be worse. Try to hold your face still. It will hurt for a little while, but you will heal."

"Halil, we owe this one no explanation," the gruff guard protested.

Halil answered his companion plainly. "She is a person, just as we are. She is new here and frightened. A little kindness will hurt no one."

"But kindness is not your place!" The gruff guard was annoyed.

There was no further conversation. The tattoo artist approached, carrying his sharply pointed stick and pot of ink.

Concubine Control

26

NANE, NOW CALLED Zehra, had spent several weeks being schooled in proper concubine demeanor. She played instruments when Volkan Karakas wanted music. She learned the dances with which he liked to be entertained.

When she was commanded to dance for him, Zehra felt dirty. She found it most difficult to repeatedly pretend that she enjoyed amusing him.

However, she was pleased that to this point he had not sought her out for sexual favors. Though Volkan had several wives and many children, he made it a regular practice to select his favored concubines for what appeared to her as rather violently painful sexual relations.

Often, he entertained his guests with concubines. These festivities always disgustingly progressed far beyond music and dancing for them. Nane rightfully feared that it was just a matter of time for her. If this was her new life, she doubted she could tolerate it.

This afternoon Zehra had finished reading poetry in French to Volkan. He seemed very pleased with her and asked her to sit just off to his side. She was not at all sure this was a good sign.

"Now, now, now Zehra," Volkan began. Hearing her slave name, Nane raised her head, but she remembered the Mother-Woman's warning and did not turn to look at him.

He continued. "Now you will see how I am taking good care of you." Volkan then clapped his hands twice.

Three guards entered, each holding the hand of one of her children. Her daughters Alin and little Arevig looked frightened. The middle child, her son Arek, thrust his chin forward and held his head high, almost defiantly.

Immediately, Nane scrambled to her feet to go embrace her babies. A eunuch grabbed her by the shoulder and pushed her back down.

Now Volkan spoke menacingly. "Ah, Zehra. You gave birth to these children, and they are lovely. But to hold them again is a reward you have not earned. Please do not worry. We give them special care in a nearby orphanage. They are receiving a proper Muslim education. And notably, we have now named them appropriately. Let us see if they are ready to great you."

Volkan rose and walked toward the children. He first approached Arevig. The youngest daughter was barely 3 years old.

"Hello," Volkan began. "What would you like to say?"

Arevig's sunny personality now flashed across her face with a smile. She pointed at Nane when she spoke. "Mama!"

The little lass immediately started scampering toward Nane. The guard scooped her up and returned her to the line with her siblings.

Volkan spoke again. "Remember, you cannot touch her unless you earn it. Let us try again. What would you like to say?"

"Mama! Mama!" Arevig started screaming. The poor baby was beside herself to see her mother again after so many weeks apart.

"It is clear that more training is needed here," Volkan scoffed.

He now turned to Alin. Nane's eldest daughter had just turned 7 during the weeks they had been separated. Volkan leaned down and hissed into the girl's ear.

"Perhaps you will remember your training. Perhaps you will deliver the message for your sister?"

Alin started to speak in Turkish, but she cast her eyes downward. "She wanted to tell you that her new name is Yaz. In Turkish that means summer. And... my new name is... Azra, which means pure."

"Verrry good," purred Volkan. He lifted his right hand to lift her long hair and toss it behind her shoulder offhandedly.

Then he ever so slowly inhaled with a lengthy hiss through his clenched teeth. "Yes, you will be very, very good. Perhaps I will keep you for my own."

Nane could no longer restrain herself. She started to rise in protest, but a guard standing nearby stepped in to stop her with a warning look. Nane looked up at him, imploringly.

In Turkish, she whispered, "Please. My daughter is just barely 7 years old."

"Shhh," he whispered back. She had often seen this guard. Halil was his name. She had observed his manner to be far kinder than most of the other guards. He was never rough with the women in the great hall. To the contrary, Halil seemed to genuinely care for the women's safety and care.

"How rare he is!" Nane thought again. She sat back down.

Volkan now stood focused on Arek, her son. Nane had noticed his tiny 5-year-old fists clenched at his sides. He clearly wanted to protest, but he displayed remarkable restraint for a little lad.

"And now you, my young boy," came Volkan's words. "You can calm yourself, boy. I won't hurt you. But you do need to show this woman what you have learned."

Arek's lips were drawn in a tight line. His eyes burned with fire. Nane watched his little chest heave as he drew in a deep breath. Dutifully, he then placed his right hand across his tummy and tucked his left hand behind his back as he performed a perfect bow, worthy of the finest courtier.

"Ahhh, very good," Volkan sneered with pleasure. "And your name?"

Arek glanced at his mother and then back at Volkan. "Arek is the name my parents gave me."

"No, no, no! You must forget the past. You are no longer a lowly pagan. You now are getting a proper education. And you have a proper Muslim name. What is that name?"

"I am not a pagan. I believe in Jesus."

Smack! Volkan's backhand across his cheek knocked Arek to the ground.

Nane wept. This was all being done to show her who was in control now. She feared for her son's life. She knew that the Ottomans were killing Armenian boys. If he did not comply...

"Please, son. Tell Master and Mama the new name they have given you." Through tears she faced her boy on the floor.

Arek swallowed... hard. The little child had spunk, but it would not serve him well in this environment. He needed to learn... fast... to survive.

"Yes, Mama," Arek murmured in Armenian. Then in Turkish he spoke aloud. "My new name is Cahill. In Turkish it means innocent."

"You will learn to listen to *me*, with no coaching from your mother," spat Volkan. "But this will do for today."

He clapped his hands. The guards began ushering the children from the room.

"But my children!" Nana implored. "I must hold them... just for a moment, please!"

"Not today. No, no, no." Volkan sneered as he continued. "You all must do better. You can never be Armenian again. You and your children are now mine. You will learn. They will do as they are told. *You* will do as you are told. Orrr... you will never see them again."

Nana hung her head. "They are all I have left in this world," she thought to herself. Then she made a solemn, silent commitment and prayer. "I will do anything this monster of a man demands. I must stay alive to keep my children safe and alive. I can do this. God help me, please."

Clandestine Meeting
27

"PSSST!" THE SOUND came from a door connecting the harem to the inner courtyard.

"One of the eunuchs turned. He saw the guard named Halil motioning to him. The eunuch stepped into the doorway.

"Do you know the slave they call Zehra?" Halil awaited the eunuch's response.

He nodded. "Yes, I do."

He turned toward the room and pointed her out across the way. Zehra sat with a sister concubine Ahu, with whom she had become friends, and another slave girl. Zehra appeared to be teaching the women some embroidery skills.

"And she is not entertaining Volkan today?"

"That is true, Halil," replied the eunuch.

Halil nodded. "Good. Please instruct her that she is to clean the glass doors in the north corner alcove. And tell her that there are children who need tending there."

The eunuch nodded and turned to cross the large common room in the harem. Halil left the doorway and disappeared down the open-air hall.

"You. Zehra," the eunuch began. Zehra looked up. "You are to go now to the north alcove doors and clean the glass and tend to some children there."

"Oh, well, yes. I can do that." Zehra put down her embroidery materials. She seemed a bit concerned.

Ahu patted her forearm and smiled. "Do not worry. I will continue our work here till you return."

"Thank you, Ahu." Zehra rose and moved smoothly across the common room toward the north alcove. As she rounded the partial wall, she saw the large 10-foot-high glass doors were open, and two girls sat on the floor. Though their backs were to her, Zehra recognized them instantly.

"Alin! Arevig! Oh, this is wonderful!"

She threw her arms around the girls. Alin gasped, and little Arevig cried out.

"Shhh!" Zehra whispered instinctively. She looked over her shoulder to see if anyone else was observing this reunion. She quickly whispered, "How did you get here? How did you find me?"

"I brought them." A deep male voice spoke from just out of sight outside the glass doors.

Zehra gulped for a breath as panic rose in her throat. Then Halil stepped into view. He held his index finger to his lips, indicating they should remain quiet.

He continued. "I could not bring your son, but he is safe. I knew the girls might blend in with the other daughters here in the harem. I must get them back to the orphanage soon, however, before their absence is noticed."

"Bless you," Zehra said, hugging her daughters again. Then she turned her full focus to the girls.

"It has been two months since I saw you with the Master. Are you well? Are they treating you kindly?"

Alin spoke first. "We are learning all that we can. And we are listening to our teachers and trying to do everything they ask."

"This is good," Zehra said. "So, what have you learned?"

"They teach us that it is most important now to only believe in the True Religion. No more pagan Christianity is allowed, or they say we will be in trouble."

Zehra's chin dropped. "Sweetheart, Christianity is not pagan. Still, you must do as they ask, but do not forget. Jesus Christ was more than a great prophet. He is the son of God."

"No. We must now only say, 'Praise Allah,' Mama."

"I understand. Good. This will keep you safe. Do whatever you must do to stay safe. Mama will always love you."

Zehra sat with her daughters, hugging them and chatting. But all too soon, Halil returned.

"I am afraid Zehra that it is time for the secret visit to end now."

"Oooh! But I do understand. I wish they could stay with me here... with all the other children."

"That is a privilege only for the wives of Volkan. And any babies you bear here, regardless of whether they are males or females. All children from your past are placed in an orphanage to learn proper Turkish skills and Muslim teaching. When the girls are old enough, Commander Volkan Karakas will select a proper Turkish family, and then the girls will marry."

"Oh, dear," sighed Zehra. "And what of my son. Is there any chance I could get a special visit with him?"

"I cannot bring a son of a slave here to the women's quarters without drawing much attention. Please know that he was only allowed to live because he is so young, and they can guide him away from the pagan ways and into the True Religion."

"So, if a male converts to Islam, he can live?

"Sometimes. Not always, but sometimes."

"And what becomes of him when he grows up?" Zehra had almost been afraid to ask.

"He will..." Halil hesitated before continuing. "Most likely, he will be trained to become one of the Commander's guards."

Zehra nodded her understanding. She helped the girls stand up and gave them both a hug.

Halil continued. "This meeting must be kept a secret. Commander Karakas would be furious. But if all goes well, I will try to arrange for you to... ehh... clean these north alcove glass doors every month or so."

"Oh! That would be wonderful!" Zehra continued. "I will be forever grateful. But I know that you are taking a great risk doing this. Why do you help me?"

"Allah teaches us to be kind and to treat others with respect."

"Hmph!" Zehra retorted. "Obviously, not everyone else follows this kindness teaching."

"Well, there are many interpretations of the Quran. But, as you Armenians say, 'Friendship is not born of words alone.' This is the right thing to do."

With that, Halil escorted Alin and Arevig out the glass doors. Zehra closed the doors behind them.

"Ahem! Zehra, you take a great risk." Ahu stood at the alcove opening into the common room.

"Uhh... I was just cleaning the glass on the doors." Zehra lied poorly.

"Of course, you were." Ahu's eyebrows curled with concern.

"Oh, Ahu! What am I going to do?"

"You are going to be the best little concubine you can be. Period."

"But my children!?!"

"Please, Zehra," implored Ahu. "You must listen. We do best when we remain quiet and do as we are told and *only* what we are told. The children were born to you, but they are now the children of Allah. Master Volkan is not known for kindness nor understanding. If he learns you are secretly seeing them, it will go very badly for you... and them."

"Oh, dear." Zehra shook her head in dismay.

And yet, Ahu's well-intended warning was not heeded. The secret meetings continued, almost every month. Ahu found herself covering for Zehra's little absences. Zehra seemed so happy after their meetings.

Finally, nearly a year later, the worst came to pass.

Caught in the Act
28

VOLKAN SWEPT INTO the main chamber of the harem. Everyone was aghast, as his mood was threatening. His nostrils flared, his brows were deeply furrowed, and flames erupted from his eyes.

He paced furiously around the room looking at each and every woman. At long last, he seated himself in a chair at the center of the room.

Volkan clapped his hands twice. Guards entered dragging a badly beaten guard between them. They dumped the limp body at Volkan's feet. As guards were not typically permitted within the harem, they then immediately retreated to the doorway. Then two of the eunuchs approached carrying long lengths of rope.

Commander Karakas kicked the prostrated guard. His wounded body flipped loosely to his side as he quietly moaned in pain.

Horror! It was Halil, the kindly guard.

Zehra gasped, but she sat very still beside Ahu. They held each other's hands as Zehra trembled in fear. She had seen the Master's eyes squint particularly harshly at her as he had initially perused the women in the room. Now she deeply feared what may loom just ahead.

At long last, Volkan spoke. His tone hung low and menacing.

"Well... well... well," he very slowly began. Before speaking again, he made the now familiar sound that cut fear through all the women. He inhaled with that slow menacing hiss through his tightly clenched teeth. "You have been getting yourself into trouble here at my harem, have you not, Halil?"

"I am sorry, Commander," Halil uttered weakly. "I meant no harm."

"Tsk, tsk, tsk. That is hardly the truth. If you defy me in any way, you do me grievous harm. If you even speak to my concubines, you do me harm. And *you*, my *trusted* guard, have done so... much... more."

"My humble apologies, Commander. It will not happen again."

"Ah, that is true. But it already *has* happened. And now I learn that this has happened regularly. And you have not just... been... speaking, have you?"

Halil did not respond. The silence that followed was utterly deafening. The tension only increased as Volkan repeated his creepily hissing inhaling through his clenched teeth.

Volkan clapped his hands again. A side door opened, and two more eunuchs entered, roughly pulling two children behind them.

Zehra's eyes widened as she watched the little boy and girl placed beside Halil. They trembled noticeably, but to Zehra's surprise, these were not *her* children!

Perhaps Halil had been secretly helping another slave reunite with her children, too.

All questions were soon answered, as one of the eunuchs then crossed the room and pulled a beautiful young concubine to her feet. Tears already were sliding down her abundantly tattooed cheeks. The eunuch then pushed her to the floor in front of Volkan and slapped her hand hard as she immediately reached out to her daughter.

Volkan then began. "Oh, concubine of mine, when was the last time you saw these little waifs?"

The woman shook her head before speaking meekly. "It has been two years, I believe. Perhaps longer."

She again reached her hands imploringly toward her children. The eunuch again gruffly pushed her back.

"And now you must know that you will never see them again, not for the rest of your miserable, worthless life. I can simply have them killed, right here before your eyes. No, that would not do. I rather you be tormented forever. So, here is what we will do. As they leave this chamber today, they will be separated from each other and adopted into good Muslim families... far, far away from here."

The aching woman looked at her children, knowing that this would be the last time she would ever see them. But they did not even glance her way. Both children simply stared down at their own feet.

Uncontrolled sobs came from the woman. The eunuchs removed the children from the chamber without further protest.

"Hush, pagan! Did you honestly believe your actions would go unpunished? You are not only out of my favor, but you will no longer enjoy the protection and comfort of my harem. You will have no more pretty things to wear. You will no longer live here. You will putrefy on the streets like the gutter rat you are.

"Your tattoos show that you belong to me, and now my people will not have anything to do with you. *Your* people will not have you either... not that any of your kind remain alive in your former village anyway. You have no soul. You are forever banished."

With that, the eunuchs removed her bracelets, coin-adorned aigrette headdress, and veil. They then roughly removed her robe, dress, and sandals.

Nudity in front of the other women of the harem was not unusual. But this was very different. The poor woman stood shrouded in shame. The eunuchs then paraded her around in front of all the other women before leading her out of the harem and across the inner courtyard. They literally discarded her on the ground outside the back gates.

Zehra swallowed hard. She looked at Ahu. But there was no time to ponder any further. Volkan was now focused solely on Halil.

"Did... you... think...," Volkan began with a threateningly slow-paced delivery. "Did you imagine that you could simply take one of my women without repercussions?"

"No, sir," Halil stated simply. "We did nothing more than kiss. We did not mean to fall in love."

"Ahhh, of course. So, perhaps you harbored the gross misconception that you and she could somehow run away and have a life together. Fools! The only remaining question regards your punishment. I could banish you, but you would only seek out my disgraced concubine. No, that would never do.

"Sooo... I could remove your lips, so there would be no more mere kissing. Hmph! In all seriousness... hmmm... shall I turn you into a eunuch or force you to become my lover?"

Volkan rose and began slowly pacing around Halil. He sneered and hissed. Finally, he waved at a couple of the eunuchs.

"Mehmet! Kemal! Strip this traitor and tie him to the stone bench... with his male parts upward."

"No! No, please!" Halil implored desperately. "Kill me, but spare me that knife, please, Commander!"

"Ah, but you did not spare me *my* grief. I shall not deny you yours."

As the eunuchs tied his naked body to the bench, Volkan continued. "No one may look away."

All the women had indeed turned their faces to the walls. No one wished to witness whatever torture their Master had in mind for the kind guard.

As they turned to face the center of the room, the women could not help but marvel at Halil's attractive form. A most masculine male, his muscles rippled throughout his naked body, which now glistened with sweat.

"Yes, this is a good idea. You now beg for my forgiveness. Well, as your beloved Armenians say, 'At death's door a man will beg for the fever.' You, Halil, will beg me for mercy. And you will never have sexual relations with any woman, ever again. But since you seem to like being around my harem, we can simply remove your male parts and let you officially join my other eunuchs."

Halil closed his eyes. He offered a silent prayer to Allah.

Volkan continued to pace around the bound, helpless guard. "Look at you," Commander Karakas cooed with a low growl. "You truly are a superb specimen of a male."

With that, Volkan gruffly grabbed ahold of Halil's genitals, squeezing hard. The tortured man squelched a painful yelp.

"Nooo," oozed Volkan. "It would not do to turn you into a eunuch. Mehmet. Kemal. Flip my 'loyal guard' onto his belly. Tie him down with buttocks at the very edge."

The eunuchs followed his instructions. Halil resigned himself to his fate. Volkan repeated his classic inhaled snake-like hiss through clenched teeth.

"Yes," he seethed, as he prepared to compromise the kind guard. "This is better. I will now treat you as a concubine. Perhaps then you will learn that I... am... your master."

Zehra closed her eyes. All the concubines and wives shuddered.

Time
29

TIME PASSED VERY slowly... painfully so. Zehra endured each day with as much courage as she could muster. She danced, though it made her feel nasty. She read poetry to him in both English and French, but she would have preferred to curse at the Master. And she politely entertained Volkan and his guests, as commanded, but her body began to pay a dear price. Sores began to appear in very personal places.

Secret meetings with her children had never happened again, but she was grateful that the Master had somehow seemed to have forgiven Halil, who had since returned to his guard duties. Of course, he was never again permitted anywhere near the section of the complex with the harem. Regardless, managing to stay in the good graces of Commander Karakas protected her children and prevented her from being banished to the gutters.

Indeed, over time, Zehra seemed to have developed a sort of sexual disease. She had not born any more children for Volkan, but her illness relieved her of the regular concubine duties, other than reading to the Master or playing music. In truth, Zehra felt oddly grateful to still live in the harem, but her primary work now was as a mere slave. When she worked in the kitchen, those days felt like blessings.

Suddenly, one morning an undeniable commotion erupted in the harem. The Great War had ended. This they already knew. The Ottoman Empire had lost. This they also knew, along with the fact that famine and disease had taken even more lives than military actions. But now, everyone had been summoned from the harem into the commander's Great Chamber.

Volkan sat on a cluster of pillows on a large chaise, as usual. What was not usual was the presence of soldiers. A ranking officer was poised to speak.

"This is a time of great confusion. There are treaties and changes. Sultan Mehmed's successor, Mehmed VI has relinquished all power. Commander Volkan Karakas now holds no sway over any of you."

Audible gasps were heard throughout the room. No one had even sensed this was coming.

"All slaves and wives who were forced to convert to Islam since November 1914, have officially had those conversions reversed. Should you wish to remain Muslim, you may now take the proper steps for conversion. But all those forced by the Ottomans to convert are now Christians again. This policy applies not only to Armenians, but to the Brits, Assyrians, and Greeks among you, as well.

"Further, we are taking Commander Karakas into our custody. He is among those under arrest for crimes committed under the shadow of the Great War.

"And, finally, from this moment forward, all slaves in this household are to be set free. Depart today... immediately. That is all you need to do to accept. If you choose to remain, you will become part of the new commander's household. That is all."

"Excuse me, sir," one of the guards spoke. "Are there any rules as to what the slaves can take with them, if they choose to leave?"

"Yes," came the reply, without hesitation. "They can take whatever they had when they arrived. All property and goods taken from Armenians must now be returned. The same will pertain to all other slaves, too."

Zehra looked at Ahu. She knew that none of them had anything but the clothes they had been wearing when they were kidnapped and sold. And all their original clothing had been donated to local orphanages years earlier.

The Turkish soldiers with the officer now escorted Volkan from the room. He did not make eye contact with anyone, not even any of his wives nor his own mother. Zehra thought this was, perhaps, a fitting sort of justice for the commander, for as the saying goes, "When the thief has stolen from a thief, God laughs in heaven."

The eunuchs and concubines now spoke rapidly with each other. All of this was totally unexpected. No one was prepared for what to do next.

"Will you stay or leave?" Ahu posed her question to Zehra.

"Well," Zehra began. "I have nowhere else to go. However, my children are out there someplace. They are just 5 years older than when I last saw them."

"But Zehra, remember that you are not well. You may need care yourself soon."

"Gracious! I cannot think about that now. My children are 8, 10, and 12 years old at this point. With every bit of strength I have left in my body, I must commit myself to finding them."

"I understand. And I respect you for your unwavering love." Ahu continued. "Please remember, Zehra, that your tattoos will cause even our own people to reject you."

"Ahh, you presume any of 'our people' remain alive."

Ahu sighed. "In truth, I have no idea what the outside world is like at all. Remember, I have been here even longer than you... my entire life."

"I know, my dear friend, but I do remember freedom. I do not know what I will find on the streets beyond these walls. But I will depart from this place with great haste. I will thank God to leave this hell behind me."

Ahu shook her head. "I have nowhere else to go. I must remain."

Zehra took Ahu's hand. "Dear friend, you may come with me. We can face whatever is out there together." Zehra nodded her head, offering Ahu encouragement.

"Zehra, I wish you all the very best. But I will remain here. I may even convert properly to Islam. I am tired. All I want is a sense of calmness and peace in my world. Perhaps I will now find it here."

"I will miss you, Ahu. You have helped me and protected me, even when it put your own safety at great peril. I will be grateful forever. But I cannot stay. As long as my health will permit, I must seek my children. I do not even know how many orphanages exist here in Constantinople, but I will use my last dying breath to find and visit them all.

"I will miss you with all my heart, Zehra."

The two women hugged. They even shed more than a couple of tears.

"Ahu, I will remember you most fondly, always."

"Attention!" The commanding voice interrupted the many conversations and farewells taking place around the hall.

"It is time for all those who are departing to remove all jewelry, adornments, and clothing that was not yours when you arrived. Place all items in the baskets around the room before departing."

Zehra gave Ahu a final hug. Ahu helped her gently remove her decorated headpiece. Other than that, she wore only a sheath of plain cloth and not even a pair of sandals.

As she joined the departing throng, Zehra realized that none of them were being allowed to leave with anything. Existing in the harem under the wickedness of Volkan, she had long ago lost all sense of shame or modesty. She knew she would find a church or an orphanage and something else to wear there.

Zehra slipped her sheath off, lifting it over her head. Before stepping through the door, she felt the hands of a guard in her hair, removing her hair combs.

Her long locks tumbled down to her waist. She lifted her chin and stepped fully naked into the sunshine on the street. Zehra smiled broadly now. Freedom was worth any price.

Bittersweet Endings
30

SADLY, ZEHRA... NANE... only had a couple of years left to live. The sexual illness brought on by her forced life in the Commander's harem only left her time to unsuccessfully search for her children. Happily, she also had the good fortune of reuniting with her younger sister, Nazeli, now known by the Turkish name Emine.

Call her Nane or call her Zehra. Call her sister Nazeli or call her Emine. With time and life's experiences, they both had learned to see past these nuances. Their given Armenian names versus their adopted Turkish names seemed far less important than the fact that they were now surrounded by loving and caring people.

Now, as Nane lay comfortably in a cozy bed in the home of her sister and brother-in-law, Aydin, she finally felt a sense of peace. Paralysis had begun overtaking her legs, but her sister doted on her endlessly.

Aydin had assisted in the continuing search for Nane's children. Unfortunately, they could find no word on where any of them had gone. Their names may well have been changed again when they were adopted by a Muslim family... or families. Everyone hoped and prayed that they were now growing up in a nurturing, kind household.

"May I ask you a question, dear sister?" Nane's voice grew increasingly weak.

"Of course, you can. Anything."

"At the harem, they told me that my tattoos show that I no longer belong... that I am not Armenian. Not Christian. Not Muslim. That I have no soul. Do you believe this is true?"

"Nane, I most certainly do not. They can force needles and ink into your skin, but they cannot force Jesus Christ out of your heart. And our souls are untouchable, no matter what anyone may do to our bodies."

Emine was firm in her convictions. She continued. "When our family was ripped away from me, I thought I was going to die. There was so much death and inhumanity around me. But I was blessed to have Muslim family friends risk their own lives and safety to save me. In marrying Aydin, I found another blessing. He is a gentle, kind husband and loving father. He never once tried to force me to convert to Islam, so I do not mind being called by my Turkish name, Emine. Aydin protected me and respected my faith. This world needs more people like him.

"Never forget that God loves us. He does not blame us for anything. He forgives us for everything. You will see, dear sister. In Heaven, He will wrap you in his loving arms. All the pain and loss you have endured will be over."

Nane smiled slightly. "Do you remember Mama's gold wedding ring?"

"Of course, yes. The three gold bands, with the two outer ones featuring hands that clasped over the entwined hearts on the center band. Why do you ask now?"

"I remember how she would gently touch that ring whenever Papa was away. He had always told her that the ring symbolized his love holding her close no matter how far apart they might be. Somehow... I feel that now. It's as if Papa is calling to me... and I feel... safe and loved."

"You are safe and loved, my dear sister. Our hearts are forever entwined, just like on that precious ring."

Nane's eyes were closed now. She then whispered her last words for the night.

"Let me eat, let me sit, and when it gets dark, let me sleep." Nane looked so peaceful.

A few tears slid down Emine's face. They had endured so much... not just her family, but all Armenians, Greeks, Assyrians, Kurds, Jews, and Turks.

"When will power-hungry men stop wreaking havoc in this world?" Emine quietly posed her question to no one in particular, since Nane now slept.

Unbeknownst to her, Aydin had been standing along the wall by the doorway. He placed his right hand on her shoulder.

"Not soon enough. Not soon enough." Aydin's words were simple but true.

He continued speaking as he walked his wife to a favorite bench in their garden. "And I wish I could guarantee that the new Turkish republic will do much better, but I just do not know. They are already making it unlawful to speak of the Armenians. They have given Armenian lands and homes to Muslim families. They are continuing to strike Armenian names from books and maps and replacing them with Turkish names. Sadly, they seem to be trying to rewrite history to even make it appear as if the Ottomans were here first, and the Armenians arrived as unwanted second-class citizens."

Emine shook her head sadly. "Seriously, why do they do these things? The Ottoman injustices and crimes need not be claimed as theirs. But trying to pretend that we Armenians were not living throughout Anatolia for thousands of years will not make it so. People will remember."

"Well, dear," Aydin continued. "If we cannot speak of it out loud, how can people be expected to learn the truth, never mind remember? As you well know, the Ottomans tried to silence the Armenian voice altogether. They reigned in this region for some 600 years, I know. For most of those years, bloodlines mixed, though not necessarily by Armenian choice, I realize. If our new leaders simply thought about this for a moment, I believe they would recognize that by now there is likely Armenian blood in all of us."

"Aydin, those words could get you arrested! Please tell me that you have not expressed such thoughts outside of this house!"

"Only in the smallest, forward-thinking circles. You see, Ottoman philosophy taught us that by converting a Christian to Islam, their blood somehow changed also. The same was believed if they had an Armenian woman bear their child. They thought that child was totally Turkish and not Armenian. Period."

Emine nodded. "Well, in theory, I understand somewhat. We Armenians tend to marry only other Armenians. However, if someone has even a little Armenian blood, we embrace them as Armenians."

"Yes, but Armenians never set out to destroy other people who did not choose to be Armenian."

"Ah, but Aydin," protested Emine. "I know there were some Armenians who retaliated against the massacres. Anger was fierce, even if warranted."

"If only the Ottomans had respected people who were not Muslim, decades of distrust and violence could have been avoided. Believe me, there are plenty of us Turks who know that the Young Turks had an official plan to eliminate Armenians and other Christians, and they tried to mask it as mere preventative tactics against a feared Armenian rebellion. We know that the Armenians lived peacefully, although always prepared to defend themselves. Just take our families as an example. Armenians had many friends who were

Turkish, Kurdish, Greek, Jewish, and Assyrian. Armenians tried to seek peace."

"I know what you say is true, Aydin. My own family was part of the effort to help refugees, while also planning for possible defensive action. Peace was all we wanted. It was the Young Turks who would not hear of it. The party of Union and Progress. Phooey. There was no unity, and there was no progress."

"Emine, please take heart when I tell you it is well known that in your city of Van, the Armenians who stood against the Ottomans who were trying to deport them had many Muslim friends, such as my own father and mother. And Armenians helped Muslims, like my family, to escape when the fighting erupted. Amidst constant cannonball attacks, the Armenian resistance begged the Turkish troops to understand that their fight was not with the Turks or any other Muslims. It was only with Van's Governor Djevdet Bey. Unfortunately, because he was the brother-in-law of the Minister of War, Pasha Enver, there was nothing your family or any other Armenians could have done to stop him from carrying out the Minister's sinister mandate. He had personally given the written orders for deportation or slaughter.

"Please know Emine, my father was disgusted to be associated with the Ottoman military. He reminded me that all we Turks had needed to do was to stand up to our government gone crazy. If we had, many of us may have also been slaughtered by the Young Turk leaders, but in the long run, years of distrust, violence, and destruction could perhaps have been prevented."

"Don't be so hard on yourself, my dear Aydin," Emine began. "A king must be worthy of a crown, and we suffered many unworthy Ottoman leaders. It was not your fault, nor the fault of most Turks that any of the bad times happened. However, trust once destroyed is very difficult to rebuild."

"Well, Emine, we are hardly helping in that regard. Our new government is following the old government's path by insisting we cast the blame on the Armenians. They are denying the massacres were unwarranted and unprovoked. In fact, they are also spreading tales that it was the Armenians who were slaughtering innocent Turkish families. Nice way to cast blame elsewhere for their crimes against our own people."

"Try not to be so troubled by that, Aydin. The world knows the truth... at least the world outside of Turkey. The facts will only become increasingly difficult for our government to deny. You are particularly aware because you were here. Your family was here. But what will happen in the next generation? And the one after that? Good people will only believe what they are told they should and must believe, even if it is utterly false. And if the people now are not being permitted to speak the truth, that silence will echo forward with great fervor."

"Dearest Emine, you are right. This is why we raise our children to be open-minded to the truth, not just the government's preferred revision of the truth. However, we must always be mindful to teach our children to be cautious about verbalizing true history in public circles, I understand. But I want them to know without a doubt what the Ottomans did to their own people. Such evils must not be permitted to pass unacknowledged forever. If they are, then any future regime, anywhere in the world, can do as it pleases with people it may choose to disrespect.

"Sadly, I fear, government leaders often pretend to be doing what is right for a nation's people and the good of all, when in truth, they are lining their own pockets while winning public favor by telling lies. And they do this at the expense of their own people... never mind their own souls. To allow leaders to spout off as if they are all-knowing and we are mere fools in need of their tutelage is foolhardy. Those in power become very wary, even jealous of hardworking people and society's brightest minds. They do not want the masses to have either wealth or education, so they paint both as very dark and untrustworthy."

"But Aydin, with the passing of time, people do forget. Pain lessens. Harsh memories soften. We are taught to forgive."

"I know, I know. Still, I think it would be best if you and I spent some time writing a few things down. And we should do this before our harsh memories totally soften."

"I... am not so sure. Would this not anger the new republic? If they do not allow the massacres of Armenians to be even mentioned, I hardly believe they would condone us writing about it."

Aydin reached for her hand. He raised it to his lips and gently kissed her palm before speaking again.

"I am so deeply sorry that your family suffered so much pain and loss. I am sorry you lost your fiancé. I am sorry the Ottoman soldiers then crumbled the once lavish city of Van to rubble. And yet, if all these things had not happened, you would not have been brought to me. Our path to each other is not one I would have chosen for you to have had to follow. But I am oddly grateful, for it led you here. And your intelligence and compassion capture my heart every bit as much as your love and your beauty."

"Oh, Aydin."

"No, I am serious. Yes, I am certain that we should write down details that have happened, so we won't forget or let the memories diminish. But you are also correct. We cannot share these things openly. From all that I have heard, I fear that even our new and more tolerant republic sees remembering negative parts of our history as illegal, at best... and treasonous at worst.

"Let us write our memoirs... letters to each other perhaps. No, wait! What if we write letters to the children? We can talk with them as they grow about all these things, but if we put details in letters for them to read later, they will also know that their conversation memories are accurate. These are treasures we can leave to future generations."

"Thank you, Aydin. You represent the very best in people, and I deeply appreciate your open-minded awareness and sensitivity. As a people, we must never forget all that has happened."

A Letter from Mama
31

DEAR ADLEE AND Sidika,

Through letters, your father and I hope to leave you some perspective on the times in which you were born. Our lives have followed some fascinating and some highly disturbing paths. Since discussing these things outside the home has been forbidden by the new government that arose following the Ottoman Empire losing the Great War, we fear you might not be permitted to officially learn the truth. Our letters may help fill in any gaps in your awareness and reinforce information from various conversations we all shared as you were growing up.

Your father was a dear friend of my big brother, Aram Gulumian during our childhood back in Van, Armenia near our sacred Mount Ararat. So, our families spent a great deal of time together. Yes, my dears. Turks and Armenians lived easily beside one another. We lived in our own quarters, as was traditional, but we all got along beautifully.

After your father moved to Constantinople, we lost track of his daily life, but his parents... your grandfather and grandmother Raffi... remained in Van and kept us up to date a bit. We were all dear friends.

When the troubles for Armenians became especially dire in 1915, my family had planned to flee, either to Yerevan further to the east or north to Kars in Russia.

My Papa was active with the Armenian resistance. He hosted a number of clandestine meetings where defense options were discussed. Defending our homes and our city would not be easy, as the government had ordered all Armenians to surrender all weapons. Unfortunately, this made it very easy for Ottoman troops to destroy town after town even in regions with very large Armenian populations.

Most of our efforts were in gathering food, clothing, and supplies for survivors of the fires and destruction of other villages and provinces. One early morning, Papa and my grandfather were returning home from helping refugees after one area had been destroyed. Along with their three fellow merchants, they were ambushed just outside our walled city of Van. All but one man was executed, leaving the one to return to the city and spread the word that the Ottomans were coming for us. Armenians would not be allowed to live.

My twin brother was very sickly, and his growth was stunted. For this, he was not permitted to serve in the military when they conscripted all the Armenian young men into the Ottoman Army. All male youths were in danger of being murdered, so they could not grow up and seek reprisals. As disguises, Mama had dressed Vahram and our baby brother Hrant like little girls.

We were awaiting Papa's return, as he was going to help us leave the city before he and Grandpapa joined the others in efforts to protect our homes and city. Mama had buried many items in our walled courtyard, so they would be there upon our return. Other larger items, such as furniture and our musical instruments were being held by Turkish friends, including your Grandfather Raffi.

That would matter little, however. Even Turkish residents were eventually forced to evacuate all of Van during the fighting or afterward, so the Ottomans could destroy it.

And it all mattered even less when soldiers came to our door. With brutes holding back Mama and our disguised brothers, my sister and I were viciously attacked.

Your Aunt Anush was a strong-spirited girl. You would have loved her, as she was often very funny, too. On that day, there was nothing to make anyone smile. Throughout the attacks, my sister never stopped fighting for even one second. Regardless, after dishonoring us both several times, the soldiers shot us and left us for dead.

Mama and the boys were forced into a large group that was allegedly being deported. However, your Grandfather Raffi had learned that everyone in the deportation group was scheduled to be slaughtered shortly after they left the walled city. He was able to warn Mama and begged her and the boys to run away before getting to the city walls.

He also promised her that he would reach our clerics and tend to our bodies. But he then discovered that I was still alive. Your Turkish grandfather risked his own life and his family's safety by taking me into their home. He and your grandmother then nursed me back to health. They renamed me Emine, so my Armenian name Nazeli would not give our secret away to the Ottomans.

At the time, I had been engaged to marry the son of one of Papa's merchant friends when he returned from Ottoman military service. But Grandfather Raffi then learned that Toros Kherbekian's entire Armenian military contingent had been lined up in a field and shot. It was only years later that we learned Toros had managed to survive and later married the Armenian woman who had helped my mother escape and also nursed Toros back to health in the Armenian underground.

We also learned that my mother... Aghavni Samargian Gulumian... and my two brothers... Vahram and Hrant, did escape from the deportation line. They even made it outside of the city. Unfortunately, Grandfather Raffi then was told that soldiers had later tracked them down and killed them.

Though it sounds bleak, I was not the only one of your Armenian family who lived. My two eldest brothers had made it to America years earlier. The eldest, Ohannes, worked hard and earned our passage to join them, but we had not managed to escape to be able to do so.

Aram, our second oldest brother, was studying at an American University. We have been unsuccessful in trying to locate them. We just know they live somewhere outside the city of Boston in America.

We likely could have learned their whereabouts in America, except that we could also not find Misag Minassian. He was one of Papa's merchant friends and our contact in Kars, Russia. Suddenly, not only was I orphaned, but we could not locate any of our contacts.

During the troubles, we also lost contact with our eldest sister. Nane had married Armen Petrosyan and moved to Constantinople. We learned she had borne three children, a boy Arek and two girls, named Alin and Arevig. Sadly, we lost track of them after the wide-scale massacres began. Only recently did we find her, as she was nearing her finals days, due to illness.

Soldiers had arrested and released her husband, but they later came to their home and murdered him. Nane was sold to be a sex slave for one of Sultan Mehmed V's commanders. They forced her to convert to Islam and changed her name to Zehra. Her children became lost to her as the commander put them in a Muslim orphanage for their conversion and retraining. The children's names were changed to Turkish names Cahill, Azra, and Yaz. We have been unable to learn their fates or locations.

So, sadly, I tell you of your Armenian family because you deserve to know that we had a hard-working family of tailors and merchants. We loved music, books, languages, and sharing time together, both in the once beautiful, ancient walled city of Van and at our summer home by the vineyards at Lake Van. We did not rebel or work against the Ottomans in any way. Just as with our forefathers, we wanted to live peacefully in the lands on which our family had lived for thousands of years.

It was not to be for us or for any other Christians. The Ottomans deliberately strove to foster hatred for Armenians, Greeks, Assyrians, and all other non-Muslims.

I thank God for our Muslim friends. They quietly, though secretly, stood by us. Your Turkish grandparents saved my life. They brought me here where we learned that I was with child from the attack by the Ottoman soldiers in our home in Van.

Please, Adlee, do not harbor hatred for the man who fathered you. He was grotesquely misguided, and his behavior was evil, I do understand. God will be his judge.

But without that horrifying chapter in my life, we would not have you. So, we learn to accept the life God provides. Always know that your true father is the one who loves you and Sidika and raised you both. He is the good man who took me in and married me despite the dire circumstances that brought me to his door.

He took great care when he named you both. Sidika means truthful. Adlee reflects that only Allah can judge, and the middle name Berat means 'the night of forgiveness.'

Yes, you are both truly our children. We are all blessed with your father's kindness and patience. He married me with genuine love and compassion in his heart. I pray that his spirit, open mind, and loving heart will always guide your paths through life.

We have not been able to openly live with easy sharing of my Armenian background. But we hope that our blended family helps you know that there are good and worthy people in all cultures and faiths. It is our honor to love you, and we look forward to embracing the next generation, as well.

Promoting distrust of and hatred for people who are different is never a good thing. When the Ottomans spread lies that we Armenians planned an insurrection, they did so to lure Kurds and mercenaries to help them eliminate us. Understandably, the truth will bring great remorse in the future. Promoting years of inhumanity against Christians was horrible to endure, especially in our own homeland. For fair-minded people like you, it is horrible to imagine, never mind accept or acknowledge.

Witnesses from many other nations saw what was repeatedly done to Armenian villages, cities, and people across all the Armenian provinces. As the Ottoman Empire lost its lands throughout Europe and northern Africa, it escalated massacres of Christians throughout Anatolia.

The world has now spoken. Despite our own government's contrary dictates, people know of the heinous massacres and feigned mass deportations of Armenians to the deserts. And yet, it is forbidden for any of us to publicly speak of these acts. The most unsavory deeds have been stricken from books and records, while all Armenian names, credits, words have been changed to Turkish ones.

Please always remember that denial does not change reality. However, I fear there may be future generations who will grow up believing the re-written versions of history as factual.

I deeply respect your Papa for not conforming to the demands of the times. He has had to remain silent around many people, as if he accepted the drivel as facts. He has appreciated the support of his closest friends and found strength in his prayers. My gratitude is endless.

It is my wish that future generations do not forget what happened to our precious Anatolia, our Armenia. There are those who would still have the world believe we were second-class peasants with no heritage, skills, or education and no value in life nor rights.

In truth, the presence of Armenians throughout Anatolia dates back thousands of years. We were the land of Ararat and Haykin in the Bible. Armenia became the first Christian nation in the world in the year 301, more than one thousand years before the Ottomans and other Mongols first began their migrations westward from central Asia.

For 600 years, the Ottoman Empire raided and often ruthlessly ruled from its base here in our homeland of Anatolia. Most of the time, they afforded Armenians some degree of autonomy. But at other times, they lauded over the native populations as if we were there only to serve them or line their pockets with gold. At other times, we were treated even worse, as if we were cattle for sale or wholesale slaughter.

Armenians remain resilient. And we hope that you remain thoughtful and compassionate. Do not confuse the despicable acts and beliefs of your Turkish ancestors, as being your fault in any way. Mostly, the people who took part were sadly misguided. Only the leaders were vile. And they have been found and decreed guilty. But our new leaders' current efforts to deny any and all wrongdoing are counterproductive, at best. It will not help heal any of us. They think we were destroyed, but Armenia lives on in our hearts.

I hope you find room in your hearts to embrace your Armenian heritage and see it as a strength, not a curse. But, in doing so, try not to cast blame on your Turkish heritage. I repeat that the actions of past generations are not your fault.

With all the love in my heart, I remain your devoted mother always,

Mama

A Letter from Papa
32

MY DEAREST CHILDREN,

When you read these letters from your mother and me, you will be adults, likely with children of your own. We will have already discussed everything we are now sharing on paper. We write letters because we do not want anything to be clouded over or diluted by the passing of time. You will know these things are true and real, both because we have talked about them and because we are putting pen to paper.

First and foremost, you shine light in my heart each and every day. Your mother and I are fully committed to your care and safety, as well as your education.

In my youth, the Ottoman Empire did not value education, especially for females. We believe in becoming as educated as you want. Perhaps it will be in languages. Perhaps medicine. Perhaps teaching. We will support your pursuit of studies as far as you choose to go.

Much of what we share with you in our first letters is about the horrible times that people here have endured, particularly in the last decades of the Ottoman Empire. It seems that our new leaders would prefer that people not remember... not know about the ways in which the Ottomans wreaked havoc on our own people and lands.

When the Great War ended, no Turks wanted to be associated with the Ottomans, the Young Turks, or the Union and Progress party. While this was utterly understandable, disregarding the treaties signed at the end of the war and disavowing what had been done to the Armenians and other Christians was questionable at best.

I pray to Allah that one day our leaders will acknowledge the hideously inhumane things we Turks did to our Christian citizens. We cannot turn back the clock or rewrite history, and it is not any future generation's responsibility to pay retributions, but we could apologize for the actions of our ancestors.

Over the years, the Ottomans built and ruled a great Empire here. But we did it on the backs of the Europeans we conquered, the Armenians whose lands we claimed for our own, and the two-and-a-half million slaves we brought here from conquered lands in Europe and Northern Africa over 200 of our years. We also enslaved countless more right here where our new republic of Turkey stands.

As the Ottoman Empire began to crumble, our leaders pushed to make a Turkey just for Turks. Toward this end, they deported and massacred countless Armenians and other Christians to the deserts of Syria.

When your grandfather and grandmother Raffi escaped from Van, they had to join Turkish and Armenian refugees fleeing for their lives. They were fortunate to be able to board one of the many boats on

Lake Van to start their journey here. You should know that of the 400 ships on Lake Van, almost all belonged to Armenians. That means Armenians rescued thousands of Turks, including your own family. They could have simply left us to fend for ourselves amidst growing famine and pestilence, but they did not.

I was personally saddened to see hundreds of educated scholars, successful business owners, and other respected community leaders arrested, imprisoned, tortured, and, far too often, executed. Their crimes? They were Armenian.

If that sounds brutal, it is because it is true. Our leaders believed if they eliminated the head of the Christian beast, it would die. But I think they merely added passion to its heart.

We Muslims lived peacefully with a great many Christian neighbors. They were English, Assyrian, and Greek, but predominantly Armenian. Our religions and cultures clashed, but we respected each other. We also enjoyed many strong friendships.

Always think for yourselves when leaders try to tell you what to think. Only fear and insecurity drive government leaders to promote and teach divisiveness and hatred, while calling it unity and progress. They accuse others of the very acts they commit themselves.

I know that such things have gone on for many generations. I also know we Turks did not invent these evil practices. What I do not know is how long it will take to set the record straight on all that was done to the

Armenians under the veil and cover of the Great War. I hope and pray it is within our lifetime or at least during your lifetimes, our dear children.

The great prophet Muhammad taught us to respond with peace when faced with aggression and intolerance. What a peculiar twist of Fate that the Christians became the ones who tried so desperately to live with us peacefully though faced with wave after wave of unwarranted aggression and hate-filled intolerance.

I do recognize that a few incidents of reprisal took place, where bands of Armenians attacked Muslims. But Allah holds no blame for those who defend themselves after being wronged. It is only surprising that all Armenians did not fight back.

Most Muslims who died during these horrific times fell victim to famine, which raged during the Great War. As if the ongoing military chaos and authorized violence against Christians wasn't enough in our land, the Spanish Flu also claimed thousands of lives, among both military and civilian populations.

The vast majority of our Christian population simply wanted peace. That should not have been denied, especially in the lands of their forefathers for thousands of years. Whether the voices of our current or future leaders acknowledge what has been done or not, the land always remembers.

It is written, "Allah will not be merciful to those who are not merciful to humankind." May our leaders today and tomorrow find mercy in their hearts to acknowledge yesterday's evil deeds and apologize for the horrors inflicted by the Ottomans.

A humble honor became mine when my parents brought your mother to me. I had known her since she was a child and was a good friend of her older brother, Aram. My first wife had died while trying to give birth to our baby, and I never thought anyone could or would fill that gaping hole in my heart. Your mother helped me heal. My heart now overflows with love for her.

Her patience and inner strength taught me, by her example, how to be a better person. She always goes about her duties with calmness, and yet determination. I have studied her face and learned a great deal more.

Gone is the smile I recall from her youth, and the sparkle I remember seeing in her eyes and in the eyes of her younger siblings. Now, despite our beautiful family and the love we all share, I see a deep pool of undeniable sadness in her eyes.

She has always been a beautiful woman and a wonderful person. And yet, this shroud of silent sadness serves as a constant reminder to me of the bad times our Ottoman leaders caused for her and her family. And for millions of other Christians. Can your mother really forgive us? Can any Armenian ever forgive us? Will future generations forgive us? Can Turks learn to forgive ourselves, or will we be denied the ability to even acknowledge our horrible deeds?

As Allah would have it, by trying to eliminate Armenians, the Ottomans were trying to eliminate themselves. For 600 years they had taken Armenian women as mothers for their children. Yes, Christian women. They forced religious conversions, but the bloodlines have mixed for centuries.

Fathering a child does not make the child's blood purely Turkish. In truth, many Armenians recognize you as Armenian if you have any Armenian blood in you. So, who among us now is not also Armenian?

We are Turkish. We are Armenian. We know that you have at least half Armenian blood from your mother. The likelihood is strong that my ancestry also includes Armenian. The same is probably true for most of us, including the heirs of our Sultans. It is well known that almost all our Sultans married and had children with non-Turkish captors.

In future letters we will address some specific stories. We want you to know about both good and bad, and there are many wonderful stories to share. We repeat these things with you in letters now to help future generations remember, too.

Our prayers for you are that you and your future families will always be loving and thoughtful. We also hope you will not always be forbidden to learn the uncomfortable truths of our times. With that, may future generations come to embrace the entwining of our cultures with pride. We are one people, we Turks and Armenians.

With all my deepest love,
Papa

The Ringing Decision
33

NURAY PLACED THE folder on the table and closed it. Cassie could hardly contain her enthusiasm.

"So, they did it. Aydin and Nazeli... I mean... Emine. They wrote things down."

Now Sidika, though growing more tired and weak, responded. "As I became a teen, my parents spoke to me of past stories. They knew what I was being taught in school. And they knew the truth was being boldly whitewashed.

"The Armenians valued education and learning trades. They worked hard. They respected women. The Ottomans led by trying to make people all the same. Some now call it Turkification. But women did not work and did not leave the house without a male relative with them. Males grew up to be in the military, or, if privileged or well-connected, perhaps in government. With most merchants, sailors, scholars, and tradesmen being Armenian, you can imagine how deeply the Armenians' success irked the Ottomans.

"Peculiar, perhaps, but it was my mother who helped me understand more clearly why the Ottomans had such loathing for Armenians in particular. There was great jealousy. The government would over-tax Christians, and it only served to make them work harder and succeed more. Mother would say, 'No one throws stones at a fruitless tree.' The Armenians were viewed as a distinct threat to Turkish images of superiority."

Nuray spoke now. "Please rest, Mama. Cassie understands."

"Yes, I do," added Cassie. "And I am forever grateful that you have shared your personal and often painful stories with me. So much time has passed."

"Indeed," continued Nuray. "In 2015, we recognized the 100th anniversary of the Ottoman's genocide of the Armenians. Yerevan hosted large remembrances of events we will never be able to forget. The word genocide did not yet exist when the 1915 massacres or the earlier Hamidian massacres or any of the other massacres took place."

"That is true," Cassie acknowledged, nodding. "Most nations of the world have made it very clear that the Ottomans actions constitute the first genocide of the modern times. And they hope for the day when current Turkish government leaders will reverse the 100 years of propaganda to deny or rewrite historic events, regardless of their grotesque levels of heinousness.

"And I know that Armenians are not the only people who have been shattered by hatred and intolerance. Just think of history! Pick a nation, any nation. Look at cultures, any cultures. And as the old Armenian proverb so aptly states, 'Where is there a tree not shaken by the wind?' Humans are humans, and we are excruciatingly slow to evolve socially."

Nuray nodded. "Just look at how Hitler's madness found him relishing the fact that the Young Turks had escaped unpunished for their foul deeds, and he clung to that knowledge to carry out his own genocide against Jews and anyone else who sympathized with their plight."

Now Nuray took her mother's hand before she spoke again. "Cassie, my mother is now 100 years old, nearly 101. Your mother is also in her 90s. They are the last of those born in the first generation after the genocide. My mother has assured me that your writing will help current and future generations know the truth, and she is most grateful that you are caring and compassionate. I am certain that your mother is also proud of your work."

"Nuray, you are right. My mother is very proud of her children. As with your mother, she raised us to study and work hard, to value honesty, and to love and to forgive. She was pleased when I published her mother's journal as a nonfiction memoir. Then, as I began writing my grandfather Hrant Gulumian's story, she asked me why I was calling it historical fiction, when the stories were true and not just based on fact. I explained that I have to add dialogue and details to which I had no knowledge or proof. That makes it fiction."

"And now," Nury interjected. "Now you have a great deal more information. How shall you use it?"

Cassie smiled. "I will finish my writing as a trilogy. There was far too much information for just one book anyway. And my historical fiction trilogy will tell the truth, including the fact that a great many Muslims helped Christians at great personal risk during the most troubled times. I know that many readers may hesitate to believe that the stories are true. And yet, that is how history plays itself out. Truth is indeed stranger than fiction."

Nuray nodded again. "Truth is truth. Denying or distorting facts does not change them. Sadly, too few people read nonfiction works, such as history books. History gets lost so easily. Or important events get barely mentioned in a paragraph or sentence. Also, we do prefer to read information from a perspective that pleases us or parallels our own philosophies.

"Though I am Turkish, I do not know how many Turks will have the courage to hear, never mind accept information that they have been told is fake for three or four generations now. They won't like it any more than realizing that our Turkish culture, and especially our 'Turkish' foods were thoroughly gleaned from the cultures of the Armenians and Greeks before us."

"Speaking of culture, our ancestors were among some very talented artisans.," Cassie said. Reaching into her purse, Cassie pulled out a small, simple box. She handed it to Nuray.

"Please take a look at this and tell me if it means anything to you... or to your mother."

Nuray opened the box and peered at the gold ring inside. She shook her head, as she then passed the box to her mother.

Sidika took one look at the ring and gasped. She gently lifted the ring from its case before speaking.

"Is it possible? Is this my grandmother's wedding ring? The one my mother spoke of so fondly. Three individual rings with a tiny bolt connecting them at the bottom. The two outer rings, each holding one of the two clasping hands...."

Sidika's jaw dropped. She went silent.

Cassie finished the sentence for her. "...the two clasping hands, that when opened reveal the entwined hearts inside. The entwined hearts of your Armenian grandfather and grandmother, Garabed and Aghavni Gulumian. Yes. This is her ring from the 1800s."

"My mother told me. She described it perfectly. The fine craftsmanship. The intricate details. She often spoke of its deep meaning. That ring became symbolic of the strength and power of their love. Grandmother Aghavni often told her that Grandpapa had said to simply touch the ring when he was away, and she would feel his love was with her always. Mama said she merely had to close her eyes and picture the ring to be able to feel the love and strength of her parents with her."

"Yes," whispered Cassie. "Yes."

Nuray now spoke. "And you have kept it all these years?"

"Of course," Cassie replied. "Aghavni Gulumian gave it to her youngest son, Hrant, when he got married.

His bride dared not wear it on her finger, as the gold is so soft. Hrant and Marjorie later became my grandparents. Since they gave it to me and started telling me the family history, it easily has been my most cherished possession."

"What will become of it now?" Nuray asked.

"I have given that a great deal of thought and consideration. This ring represents millions of Armenian stories, so I know its forever home needs to be somewhere that values and cherishes the culture and history of our homeland and people.

When the Gulumians first arrived in America, they made their way to Boston in a state called Massachusetts. There is a flourishing Armenian population there, especially in a suburb called Watertown. This city became a powerful draw for Armenians when the Hood Rubber factory opened there in 1896. By 1930, there were more than 3500 Armenians living there. In 2023, the population totals nearly 35,000. I have been long considering donating this ring to the Armenian Museum of America, which is located in Watertown."

"I hope it is a worthy place," Nuray wondered aloud.

"Oh, yes! In fact, it has become the largest repository of Armenian culture in the Diaspora. They have conserved tens of thousands of ancient artifacts, maps, medieval coins, rugs, books, and family treasures. This ring tells a story of tremendous love, faith, family, and strength. I can think of no greater resting place."

"Ah, preserving culture and history." Nuray continued. "I like your idea very much. The Armenian Museum of America makes a fine forever home."

Sidika now added, "And your books. Please include the books you write that tell the stories that blossomed from this ring. These are your family's stories, our family's stories. They are true stories that need to be preserved and never forgotten. And do not delay. As Mama used to say, 'No one is sure that his light will burn till morning.' You should act with some haste."

After a few more hours of sharing and chatting, Cassie prepared to depart for the airport to begin her trip back home to the United States. She held hands with both women as they said their emotional farewells.

"We have barely met, and yet, I somehow feel as though I have known you both forever. Thank you for inviting me into your lives. Thank you for having the courage to share your personal stories with me," Cassie began. "While I have written words from my grandfather Hrant's perspective and chronicled my own mother's life, you opened my heart to previously unknown possibilities."

Nuray nodded. "You did not know we existed. And we had not known that Aghavni and her sons had made it to America, where they all lived out their lives."

Sidika squeezed the ladies' hands tightly. Nuray and Cassie looked at her. They saw a tear slide down the woman's cheek as she spoke.

"You started your story by learning about Armenia. Following little Hrant's story led to your life in America. Joining us, we have brought Turkey into the light. Yours will be a healing trilogy that matters deeply. You will help us Turks understand that acknowledging the heinous plans and actions of our ancestors does not make them our fault, nor our responsibility. We Turks like to recognize and say that there are two sides to this story. It is time for us to now dare to accept the side that Armenians and the rest of the world already know.

"You may also help Armenians, who are still struggling with generations of pain, to find true forgiveness. I think it has perhaps felt impossible to forgive when so many Turks have been forced to live in denial.

"There will be no vindication. We cannot go back and correct the past, but some of us need more growth, understanding, and strength to finally accept as history the dark deeds that our officials have deliberately tried to hide or at least rationalize and minimize for more than 100 years. I must thank you, Cassie, for your peaceful, healing, and compassionate approach."

Cassie wrapped her arms warmly around the elder woman. "Thank you, for being the truly wonderful, open, and accepting person you are. I love you."

"As I love you, Cassie. Always know that you have brought special meaning to my life that I did not expect to find. This may sound odd, but you and your writings give me a peaceful sense of closure."

Cassie spoke again. "I will never forget you, Sidika or your exceptional strength. You dared to share some Turkish history through stories that would cause many to still scowl and openly discourage being told."

Sidika smiled wryly now. "Ah, but if an old woman cannot share her stories, how else could they become part of her legacy? Whether they be stories of mine or my friends or my neighbors, they should all be shared. This is how history weaves its complex tapestry. We must never forget even the threads that are not shiny and beautiful."

As she boarded her flight home, Cassie thanked God for the blessings from family and friends while growing up in America. She still smiled while considering all she had learned about her Armenian culture and history over the years. So many stories. So much passion and compassion.

Her thoughts spun wildly. "So much has changed. We can now cross oceans faster than we used to go to a neighboring state. Events anywhere can be seen worldwide almost instantaneously. We can now destroy cities on the other side of the planet with the touch of a button. Diseases once thought to be incurable are disappearing. Great empires have fallen, and new countries have taken their place. And yet, still, after centuries upon centuries, man's inhumanity to man continues. We fly into outer space and visit other planets, but we cannot seem to learn to tolerate, never mind respect other people and different beliefs.

As the Armenian proverb says, 'The water goes, the sand remains. The person dies, the memory remains.'"

Forget? No.

Forgive? Yes.

That is our destiny.

Invitation

Thank you for reading Book 3 in the Destiny trilogy, <u>Destiny of Daring: Never Forget</u>. If you enjoyed the book, please consider leaving a brief review on Amazon or elsewhere so others can receive the same value that you have. I take my readers' comments to heart and look forward to every remark. Honest reviews help me to write even better books for you and others to enjoy.

Thank you!

Cathy

Map Sketches

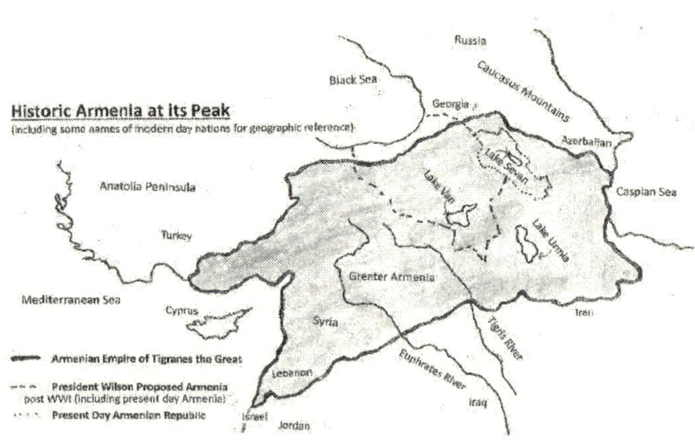

RUSSIA
SPAIN
Black Sea
Caspian Sea
ITALY
Ocean
GREECE
ANATOLIA
PERSIA
ALGERIA
Mediterranean Sea
SYRIA
TRIPOLI
Persian Gulf
EGYPT
OTTOMAN EMPIRE
& vassal states at its peak 1556
ARABIA
Red Sea
Georgia
ARMENIA
Present Day
Azerbaijan
Turkey
Yerevan
Lake Sevan
Mount Ararat
Azerbaijan
Iran

Sent to Washington, DC by Henry Morgenthau,
U.S. Ambassador to Ottoman Empire July 16, 1915

Author Ponderings

Books 1 and 2 in the Destiny trilogy tell my Armenian family's personal story. They are not just "based on a true story." They share about real people and actual events that happened in my family, both past and present. I think readers sometimes may think that historical fiction, while based on history, may contain a lot more fiction than to just add color.

For example, after Book 2's release, I received many reviewer and reader comments expressing genuine hope that Aghavni's wedding ring was real and true. Oh, yes. Now you know it very much was and is real and true.

Author with Berj Chekijian and her husband Ron Martin, presenting the ring to the Armenian Museum of America, September 2023

I was deeply humbled to take the precious ring from Aghavni Gulumian, my amazingly courageous Great

Grandmother, to the Armenian Museum of America. Director Berj Chekijian welcomed my husband and me as though we were long-time friends. And now we hope we will be.

The museum is a "must-see." The exhibits are nothing less than phenomenal. The people are superb. The work being done is absolutely state of the art.

Imagine the skill and extraordinarily detailed work to restore ancient manuscripts featuring intricate, full-color illustrations complete with gold, or to make paper to repair worn away sections of paper. This is the sort of endeavor that takes place every day.

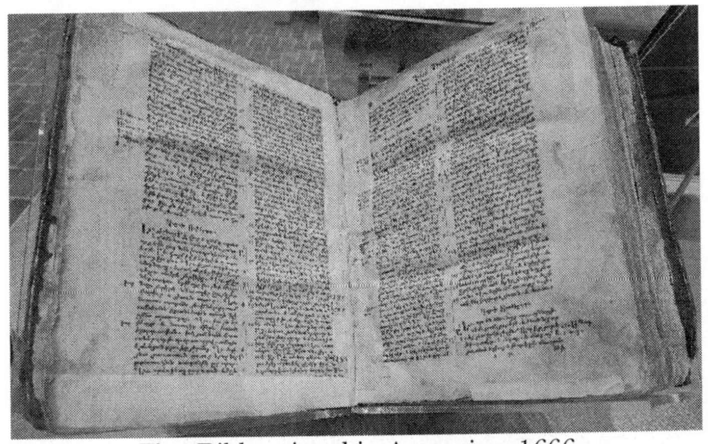

First Bible printed in Armenian; 1666

Definitely check out The Armenian Museum of America. You can visit the exhibits at 65 Main Street in Watertown, Massachusetts Thursday through Sunday from 12 – 6pm. **www.ArmenianMuseum.org**

As a 501(c) 3 non-profit organization, I know any level of support is greatly appreciated. We can all become annual members, regardless of our proximity to the museum.

I felt especially honored when Director Chekijian suggested that Great Grammy Gulumian's precious little gold trio of rings from Van, Armenia would make a perfect exhibit for their Family case, which is the first exhibit that visitors see upon entering the museum. He proposed the ring could be flanked by the Destiny trilogy of books telling our Armenian family story.

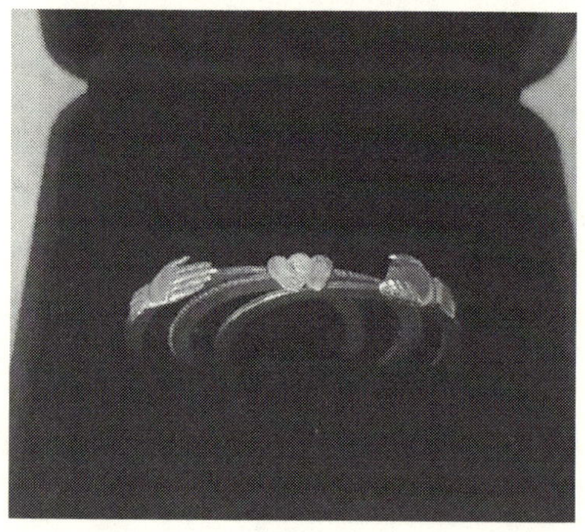

My emotional level upon leaving the Museum caught me a bit off guard. I wept. The feeling was not sadness at parting with the only Gulumian family item that made it to America. My heart was full of happiness and fulfillment, as if I could feel my own ancestors' sentiments. Somehow, I felt the embrace of them all... Aghavni, Garabed, Hrant, Marjorie... everyone.

Fulfilled is the right word. In completing the trilogy, I was also able to fictionalize stories from extended family and Armenian friends. I am especially grateful to Marian Murachanian Major, who has inspired me more than she knows. All my family and friends have my deepest gratitude for entrusting me with the sharing of their chronicles as I completed Book 3.

Sadly, challenging and disturbing stories, such as the Gulumian's saga and perhaps your own family's history, continue unfolding daily. When I compare activities of the past with some of the present, I sense that we fail greatly in our efforts toward progress.

Ghastly is the word I choose for the hypocrisy in politics that has enabled leaders of many nations, my own included, to tolerate and perpetuate many evil deeds. No widespread terror can be rightfully justified as being for the greater good, economically, socially, or religiously. No levels of intolerance and utter disrespect can be rationalized enough to make them acceptable. Evil deeds beget more evil deeds. Retaliations beget further retaliations. And, unfortunately, freedom seekers beget freedom crushers.

All civilizations struggle mightily to deal with the ugly parts of our histories, and we all have them. For example, in the United States, we have acknowledged that slavery was and is evil. However, none of us today owned plantations or bought, sold, or owned slaves in the building of our young nation. And yet, there are those who sincerely feel that today's taxpayers owe financial restitution along with social, educational, and employment preference to all descendants of anyone from Africa.

Others, of course, contend that such provisions only serve to punish businesses and people who never have practiced, nor supported slavery. Disrespecting one group to provide something of a "guilt compensation" to another group merely exacerbates the social harm.

Mankind's inhumanity to mankind has included slavery and barbarianism for thousands of years... for millennia before the 13 colonies in North America were settled. Even in Africa, tribes have been actively kidnapping and selling people from other communities as slaves for thousands of years. And our nation took part in that for over one hundred of those years.

We need not deny or rationalize our history. But just imagine if the U.S. had tried eliminating all references to slavery, slave owners, and slave trading. Suppose we had tried to rewrite history and spin it as a peaceful relocation of a minority seeking work or a fresh start in a new land.

People would have rightfully scoffed. But imagine if such revisionist untruths had become the official word, appeared in all records and history books, and were deemed as the only stories that could be legally shared. How many generations might it take before the general population started seriously believing the propaganda positions?

Just because a practice has gone on for thousands of years does not make it acceptable. And we should note that slavery... kidnapping people to sell to the highest bidder... still goes on today... worldwide. The sex slave market is grotesquely large and active. Children remain the most vulnerable victims.

However, most of the world recognizes that ownership and enslavement of another human is wrong... just plain unjustifiable. In the 21st century, this should be unfathomable.

Race relations in the U.S. remain deeply problematic. Perhaps one day we will find a way to stop beating ourselves up over our dark histories and focus on treating each other fairly and with respect going forward... regardless of our background, sex, skin color, religion, or political leanings. Perhaps.

Regrettably, I fear that we all witness great intolerance and divisiveness, especially from the very people wishing to be perceived as the most tolerant and unifying. Our human ability to be insincere often flabbergasts me.

Thus, wars continue to rage, because one people's leaders hate another people's leaders. Or power mongers need more minions to carry on their evil deeds. Or one group believes some other holds their rightful lands. All we need to do is look at current events, from Russia's invasion of Ukraine to the Hamas atrocities against civilians in Israel.

It is written, "There is no reason for war that reasonable men cannot resolve." Regardless of the nation or leaders, we seem to be dealing with reason far too infrequently.

Can we ever stop trying to claim or reclaim stolen lands? I think it's true that we all live on conquered soil. All of us. Can we stop "canceling" people with whom we disagree? Can we stop arguing about whose God is right and true? Can we stop fussing about colors and accept that we are all one race... the human race?

Perhaps one day we will be able to reject the politics of fear and control that pushes hard to force us all into one sweeping box, lauded over by those who want us to believe they are smarter and more righteous than the rest of us. If we can learn to stand together for each other, we will be able to stand against those who may still do ill against the strongest or weakest among us.

Perhaps we will learn to defend reason and freedom. To get there, however, I know that more light needs to shine into the darkest corners. Denial of past evils merely postpones full awareness.

Today's Turkish population is not responsible for the actions of its prior government. The Ottoman Empire was powerful for hundreds of years. Yes, many of its practices are seen as unacceptable and even unthinkable today. And yet, attempting to deny the existence of the planned deportations and massacres of Armenians smacks of political cover up and has done so since the Ottomans first planned, touted, and carried out that course of action.

Denials do not change history. And re-writing history only works until people are permitted and encouraged to think for themselves and learn the rest of the story from the rest of the world.

There is no cost to acknowledge the evils executed by the Ottoman military doctrines. I have learned that Kurds have openly acknowledged and apologized for their role in the holocaust against the Armenians and other Christians. Ever-increasing numbers of Turks are also acknowledging ancestral actions that we can all only wish could be undone.

We all win when our acknowledgments come with vows to never let our nations become lost again in storms of bigotry, divisiveness, and blatant disregard for other humans.

This is no different than our personal apologies to one another over anything. When sincere, they are delivered with no excuses nor rationalizations. And they are followed with actions that parallel the lessons learned.

Simmering distrust between Armenians and Turks needs to be nipped. The same is true between all races, religions, nations, and cultures that may clash.

Denials are pointless at best, especially when billions of people around the world know the truth. Denial is not a healthy practice for individuals, never mind nations. Attempts to discredit genocide evidence sources as prejudicial or dubious are made because the vast majority of sources support the reality of the Armenian genocide. The plethora of evidence hails not from ancient grievances or unsubstantiated allegations.

And stating what one wishes was the truth as if it was true is worse than wishful thinking. It inflames hatred, is deliberately divisive, and spawns more denialism, even among innocents who have not been allowed to know the truth in the first place. Attempts to discredit facts smacks of "cancel culture," which is rather twisted, since canceling Armenians was the Ottoman goal.

There are two sides to every story, indeed. And it is high time that Turkey officially allowed and encouraged the other side of the story to be told in Turkey.

Tony Dungy, a former NFL player and first black coach in the NFL to win a Super Bowl, put it rather succinctly. In an interview for the June 2023 edition of "Decisions" magazine he noted, "To those who hate the truth, it will sound like hate."

Thank you to everyone, both Christian and Muslim, who helped ancestors like mine in their struggles for survival. If we could just let ourselves be, we are one people with far more similarities than differences.

As I stated in Book 1 of the Destiny trilogy, "We are all on journeys, with many meandering and intersecting paths. My greatest wishes are that we do all we can to become more tolerant, more loving, and more worthy people along the way."

Cathy

Historical Timeline

Specific focus throughout the Destiny trilogy has been on the city of Van, because that was the base of my family history. However, Armenians and Muslims from every other Armenian province and city share similar stories and history.

2492 BC
First records of Armenian history in the Armenian Highlands.

820 BC
City of Van was founded.

782 BC
Yerevan, Armenia was founded as both a fortress and royal capitol, making it 29 years older than Rome and the oldest continuously operating capital in the world.

7th century BC
Ancient Greek historians Herodotus and Eudoxus refer to Armenia and Armenians.

5th century BC
Armenia was ruled by the Achaemenian Empire of Persia, continuing until Alexander the Great's conquest.

165 BC
Failed attempts were made to merge the eastern and western parts of Armenia into one.

65 BC (approx.)
Tigranes II (the Great) (95 – 55 BC) united the eastern and western parts of Armenia, forming the strongest state in the Roman east, lasting nearly 500 years.

34 BC

Marc Anthony invaded Armenia.

48-49 AD

Apostles Thaddeus and Barthlomew introduce Christianity to Armenia.

114

Emperor Trajan incorporated Armenia into the Roman Empire, making it a full Roman province.

301

King Tiridates the Great accepts Christianity for the Armenian people, and Armenia becomes the world's first Christian nation.

330

The ancient city called Byzantium was renamed Constantinople (now Istanbul in Turkey). Roman Emperor Constantine's "New Rome" stood as the seat of the Byzantine Empire for the next 1,100 years, until being overrun by Mehmed II of the Ottoman Empire in 1453.

331

Alexander the Great's Macedonian Empire absorbed Armenia, but Armenians continued to enjoy great autonomy.

395

The Bible was translated into Armenian.

405

Though the language existed for some 3000 years, Armenian linguist and monk Mesrop Mashtots created the Armenian alphabet in 405AD, assisted by the supreme head of the Armenian Apostolic Church, Isaac (Sahak) the Great. The alphabet was established with 36 characters (sounds); 2 letters were added later. The Bible was the first book published in the new Armenian alphabet.

536

Byzantine emperor Justinian I reorganized Byzantine Armenia into 4 provinces and suppressed Armenia's overall power.

637

The Armenian Patriarchate was established in Jerusalem.

640

The first Arab invasion of Armenia took place.

653

Armenia was surrendered to the Arabs, who granted it virtual autonomy.

1054

As the Christian church split into Roman and Eastern divisions, Constantinople became the seat of the Eastern Orthodox Church, remaining so even after the Muslim Ottoman Empire took control of the city in the 15th century.

1227

Following the death of Genghis Khan in 1227, the Mongolian Kingdom continued to spread westward. The Mongols reached the Caucasus and conquered them. Despite the religious differences, they mixed with Christian Armenian women.

1299

Ottoman Empire was founded by Osman, a Turkish tribal leader who was a descendant of a Turkish tribe that migrated west out of Central Asia following Mongold conquests.

1327

The last king of Armenia was captured, ransomed in 1382. The title "King of Armenia" passed to the kings of Cyprus and then to the Venetians.

1453

Ottoman Sultan Mehmed II captured Constantinople and declared it the capital of the Ottoman Empire. He also renamed the city Istanbul, but the world had known the city as Constantinople for so long that the name Istanbul took centuries to be widely used.

1512

Printing took place of the first Armenian books. Prior to this, books had been copied by hand onto parchments or scrolls.

1602

War broke out and Shah Abbas I fought to regain control of Armenia for Persia. In an effort to stimulate trade throughout his dominions, he forcibly transferred thousands of Armenians from Julfa to Esfahan, Iran. Those who survived the march settled in the quarter named New Julfa. Armenian merchants played an important role in the economic life of Iran, serving as links between Europe and the East. The Armenians here amassed great wealth and built many magnificent churches and mansions.

1620

With peace, most of Armenia remained in Ottoman hands. Persia retained regions of Yerevan, Nakhichevan (now Azerbaijan), and Karabakh.

1813

Russians advanced into the Caucasus, and Persia recognized Russia's authority over Georgia, Northern Azerbaijan, and Karabakh. In 1828 they ceded Yerevan and Nakhichevan.

1844

Mehmed Resad (Sultan Mehmed V) was born in Constantinople 11/2/1844 and died there 7/3/1918. The 35th (and next to last) Ottoman Sultan's reign was marked by absolute rule of the Committee of Union and Progress (CUP) and by Turkey's defeat in the Great War.

1870

Garabed Ohanes Gulumian was born in Van, Armenia, where he grew up to be a tailor and merchant, active with Armenian resistance efforts. He was ambushed and executed in April 1915 by Ottoman Turks.

1871

Aghavni Gadara Samargian was born in Salmast, Armenia. She married Garabed Gulumian in 1887 and moved to the walled city of Van. She emigrated to the United States in 1916 with her two youngest sons, Vahram and Hrant, where they joined her two eldest sons, Ohannes and Aram. She died in 1956 in Salisbury, NH in the United States.

1878

After the Russo-Turkish War of 1877-78, in which Russian Armenians had taken part, Russia insisted in the Treaty of San Stefano on reforms to protect the Sultan's Armenian subjects. The "Armenian question" remained a factor in international politics.

1879

On March 19 Aram Manukian was born Sergei (Sarkis) Hovhannisian in Davit Bek, Armenia. When he later became active in politics, he adopted the pseudonym of Aram Manukian. He later served as a leading member of the Armenian Revolutionary Federation party (Dashnaktsutyn) and was most active in Van. From 1918 until his death on

January 29ᵗʰ, 1919 he served as the Minister of Internal Affairs in Yerevan, Armenia.

<u>1895</u>

With Armenians continuing to demand the much-needed reforms, Sultan Abdül Hamid II felt compelled to promise Britain, France, and Russia that he would carry out the reforms. Instead, large-scale systematic massacres took pace throughout the Armenian provinces. These became known as the Hamidian Massacres.

<u>1906</u>

The U.S. upgraded its presence in Constantinople with an official embassy.

<u>1914</u>

The Great War (now called World War I) began on July 28.

The Young Turks entered Great War on the side of the Central Powers, signing the Secret Ottoman-German Alliance in August.

A prepared declaration on October 11 charged every Turk with the religious duty to kill three r four "infidel" Christian Armenians to please Allah. Most Muslims viewed the massacres with horror. When provincial governors refused to execute the orders that had reached them, they were immediately dismissed and replaced with compliant officials.

<u>1915</u>

On January 12 Talaat Bey Pasha, Ottoman Minister of the Interior, declared there was only room for Turks in Turkey; ordered all Armenians to turn in all weapons.

The first wave of Armenian "deportations" was carried out in February as Christians were removed from Cilicia on the northeast shore of the Mediterranean Sea.

On February 25th, the Ottomans demobilized all non-Muslim soldiers and relocated them into labor battalions.

By April 15 Armenian refugees from towns and villages surrounding the city of Van arrived and notified Van's inhabitants that 80 villages in the Van province were already obliterated. Easily 24,000 Armenians there were slaughtered over a 3-day period.

In April, the ambush and executions of Garabed Gulumian and his father, Ohanes Gulumian took place outside the walled city of Van. The two youngest Gulumian daughters were raped and shot in their home.

On April 18 Djevdet Bey (Djevdet Tahir Belbez), the Governor-General of Van demands all Armenians in the city of Van surrender all remaining weapons. The Armenians refuse, because of the attacks on the surrounding villages.

The Armenian resistance against the Ottoman Turks began on April 19 in Van, Armenia, marking one of the only acts of self-defense against the Ottoman Empire's armed forces in the Armenian genocide.

On April 19 Van province Governor Djevdet Bey issued an order for the entire province. "The Armenians must be exterminated. If any Muslim protects a Christian, first his house shall be burnt; then the Christian killed before his eyes, then his [the Muslim's] family and then himself." Following the Great War, Djevdet Bey was found guilty of war crimes for his operations in the city and province of Van during the spring of 1915.

From April 18-30 another 32,000 Armenians were slaughtered throughout the Van province, including remote villages.

On April 24th some 250 Armenian intellectuals and community leaders were arrested in Constantinople; most were later executed. Some were sent to prisons in Chankri and Ayash, where most were later slain. This date is considered the official beginning of the genocide that lasted until 1923.

Halil Pasha's Ottoman forces were defeated on May 2 by the Russian Army in the Caucuses. They retreated to Van, Bitlis, and Mush, where they participated in the ongoing massacres of Armenians.

Due to rising Western sympathies with the Armenians' plight, Halil Pasha decreed that all Armenians were "traitors against the high government," which caused civil conflict.

Aghavni Gulumian escaped from Van with her two sons, Vahram and Hrant disguised as little girls.

On May 17, the Ottomans retreated from the city of Van as the Russian forces approached.

Russian Major-General Nikolayev selected Aram Manukian as provisional governor of Van on May 19, a short-lived post that only lasted through July. Manukian then worked to organize the migration of thousands of Armenian refugees to Eastern Armenia.

On May 24, the Allied Powers (Great Britain, France, & Russia) issued a joint statement accusing the Young Turk regime of crimes against humanity and civilization.
The Ottoman Army defeated the Russian Army at the Battle of Malazgirt, Jully 10-26. As a result, the Russians evacuated

Van on August 4 to join other fronts of the ongoing Great War. More than 100,000 refugees fled, attempting to follow the Russian troops. Tens of thousands died.

On September 29 the Ottoman Army left the city of Van, and some of the Armenians who had escaped returned.

The August 4 New York Times headline read, "Report Turks Shot Women and Children." The news article continued, "9,000 Armenians were massacred and thrown into the Tigris. This included massacring all the males in Bitlis and forcing all the women and children to the banks of the Tigris River. Then they shot them and threw the bodies into the river."

George Horton, former US Consul General at Smyrna, wrote in a report to the U.S. Secretary of State, "I wish to repeat that the consistent policy of the Turks, since the fall of Abdul Hamid, has been the expulsion, killing, and extermination of the Christian races."

The Near East Relief Project was started in 1915 to address the 'catastrophic humanitarian consequences' of the Armenian massacres. Raising funds, the program set up refugee camps, clinics, and hospitals to help those displaced by the genocide. They also cared for 132,000 Armenian orphans.

1916
By the end of the year, more than 2,300 Armenian towns and villages had been obliterated.

1917
The Ottoman Empire severed diplomatic relations with the United States on April 20, after the U.S. declared war against Germany on April 4.

On October 15 Ottoman Sultan Mehmed V hosted Germany's Keiser Wilhelm II in Constantinople.

1918

By April 1918 the Russian Revolution of 1917 saw the Russian Army dissolve, and Van was totally cut off from the Allies. The Assyrians joined the Armenians who were attempting to hold the city. By April 6 the Ottomans took control again, forcing the remaining Armenians to evacuate.

From May 21-29 Aram Manukian helped organize the defense against the advancing Turkish Army stopping the Turks at the Battle of Sardarabad, saving Yerevan and preventing the complete destruction of Armenia.

On July 3 Mehmed V, the Ottoman Sultan who officially declared war/jihad against the Entente Powers (the Allies) died at age 73. His half-brother Mehmed VI succeed him on July 4, 1918, and ruled until November 1, 1922, as the 36th and final sultan.

The Ottoman Empire signed an armistice treaty aboard the British battleship Agamemnon in the Aegean Sea on October 30.

World War I, then called the Great War, officially ended on November 11, as Germany signed an armistice agreement with the Allies.

The Young Turk triumvirate... Talaat, Enver, & Djemal... abruptly resigned their government posts and fled to Germany for asylum.

The new Turkish republic continued Ottoman endeavors to obliterate what remained of Armenia. Countless cultural remnants were demolished, including priceless masterpieces of ancient architecture, old libraries, and archives. They also leveled entire cities, including Kharpert, Van, and the ancient capital of Ani in their attempts to remove the 3,000-year-old civilization.

1919

In the verdict of the Turkish military tribunal on July 5, all Ottoman officials were unanimously deemed guilty and sentenced to death, including Prime Minister Talaat Pasha, Minister of War Enver Effendi, Minister of the Navy Djemal Effendi, and Minister of Education Dr. Nazim.

1920

The Treaty of Sèvres was signed by the Allies and Ottoman Empire on August 10, recognizing the Armenian nation in Anatolia that emerged in 1918. The treaty acknowledged "the terrorist regime which as existed in Turkey since November 1, 1914." The Turkish government agreed to hand over to the Allied Powers the people responsible for the massacres. Turkey also agreed to relent to United States President Woodrow Wilson to restructure the Turkish borders. As part of his plan, the western part of Armenia included Armenian provinces of Erzerum, Trebizand, Van, and Bitlis, and he stipulated granting Armenia lands to the sea. Turkey also agreed to remove all military from any Turkish lands bordering on the newly laid out Armenian territory.

In the month of November, Turkey and Bolshevik Russia simultaneously attacked the new Republic of Armenia and partitioned its territories to suit them. Dramatically outnumbered by the Turks, Armenia lost what Turkey called the Eastern Front without a fight, revealing the complete collapse of the Treaty of Sèvres.

1922

The new Republic of Turkey's regime ignored the new partitioning that returned some Armenian provinces to

Armenia and announced new borders, which encompassed the lands that had been returned to Armenia following Turkey's defeat in the Great War.

David Lloyd George, British Prime Minister informed the British on October 14 about the great crimes against the Armenians and Greeks by the Turks, stating, "Since 1914 the Turks, according to official testimony, have slaughtered in cold blood one million and a half Armenian men, women, and children and five hundred thousand Greeks without any provocation at all."

1923

On October 29 the Treaty of Lausanne formally established the Republic of Turkey. The capital was moved to Ankara. The treaty omitted all references to Armenia and any Armenian rights.

Army officer Mustafa Kemal, who took the name Atatürk (1881 – 1938), served as Turkey's first president from 1923 till his death in 1938. His first act as to have all Armenian names removed from centuries-old records which proved ownership of land and property. The names were replaced with Turkish names. The same was done with all Armenian accomplishments. It was proclaimed that there never existed an Armenia in Turkey and said that Armenians had never lived on the land.

Armenian church records in 1914 recorded more than 2500 churches, nearly 2000 Armenian schools, and over 400 monasteries. After the Turkish destruction, barely 50 churches, 15 schools, and no monasteries remained.

1928

Now land-locked and centered only around Yerevan, what remained of eastern Armenia became a Soviet republic for

71 years, with harsh life and state terror under Joseph Stalin's rule through 1953.

1930
The city of Constantinople officially adopted the name Istanbul.

1939
On June 12 the Great War was first referred to as World War I by Time Magazine, as it called the upcoming war World War 2.

Adolf Hitler addressed his chief military commanders on August 22, just prior to attacking Poland. Statements later were used in trials for war crimes and crimes against humanity as it is said that Hitler referred to his awareness of the Armenian genocide. A documented copy of one of his two Obersalzberg Speeches that day notes a hypothetical question posed by Hitler, when he asked, "Who, after all, speaks today of the annihilation of the Armenians?"

1981
On April 22 President Ronald Reagan said, "Like the genocide of the Armenians before it, and the genocide of the Cambodians which followed it – and like too many other such persecutions of too many other people – the lessons of the Holocaust must never be forgotten."

1988
In June , Vice-president George H.W. Bush said, "The United States must acknowledge the attempted genocide of the Armenian people in the last years of the Ottoman Empire, based on the testimony of survivors, scholars, and indeed our own representatives at the time, if we are to ensure that such horrors are not repeated."

1985

Mikhail Gorbachev became general secretary of the Soviet Union, bringing in an age of reform for the USSR. Armenians organized a massive national movement.

1990

The Armenian National Movement won a majority in parliament on August 23, and Armenia declared sovereignty.

Armenia declared independence on September 23, and in October, Levon Ter-Petrossian was elected as the first president of Armenia.

2001

On April 24, U.S. President George W. Bush said, "Today marks the commemoration of one of the great tragedies of history: the forced exile and annihilation of approximately 1.5 million Armenians in the closing years of the Ottoman Empire. These infamous killings darkened the 20th Century and continue to haunt us to this day. Let us mark this year the 1700th anniversary   the establishment of Christianity in Armenia. Let us celebrate the spirit that illuminated the pages in history in 451 when the Armenians refused to bow to Persian demands that they renounce their faith. The Armenian reply was both courageous and unequivocal: "From this faith none can shake us, neither angels, nor man, neither swords, fire or water, nor any bitter torturers." This is the spirit that survived again in the face of the bitter fate that befell so many Armenians at the end of the Ottoman Empire."

2020

On July 7, U.S. President Donald J. Trump said following widespread damage of statues in the U.S., "There seems to be a lack of understanding and historical knowledge when the Armenian Genocide Memorial, remembering victims of all crimes against humanity, including slavery, is vandalized.

2021
U.S. President Joseph R. Biden said on April 24, "The American people honor all those Armenians who perished in the genocide that began 106 years ago today."

2023
Aghavni's wedding ring from Garabed Gulumian was donated to Armenian Museum of America in Massachusetts in the United States of America.

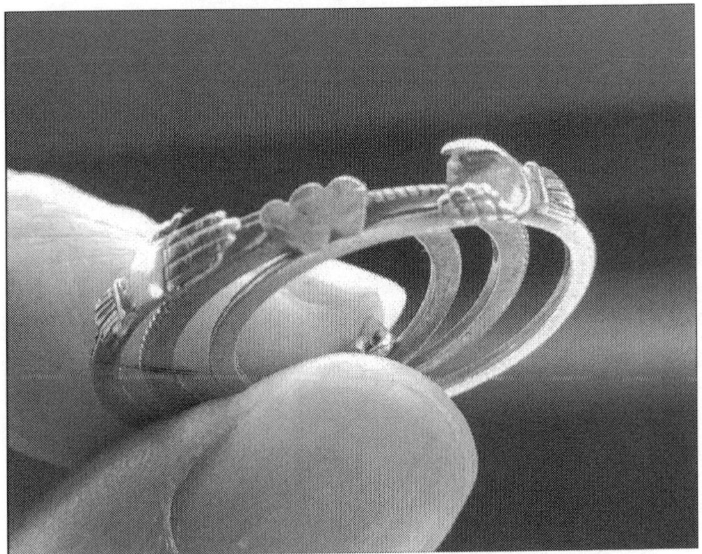

Aghavni Gulumian's wedding ring from 1887

The Armenian Population Before and After the Genocide*

Region	1914	1922
Bitlis	220,000	56,000
Diarbekir	124,000	3,000
Erzerum	215,000	1,500
Kharpert	204,000	35,000
Sivas	225,000	16,800
Van	197,000	500
Trebizond	73,390	15,000
Western Anatolia	371,000	27,000
Cilicia and Northern Syria	309,000	70,000
European Turkey	194,000	163,000
TOTAL	2,132,390	387,800

*Figures provided by the Armenian Genocide Museum, Yerevan

Photo from the Armenian Museum of America
Data from the Armenian Genocide Museum, Yerevan, Armenia

Armenian Proverbs and Sayings

For thousands of years, Armenian religious leaders and educators used parables and ageless expressions to teach life lessons in one of the world's most ancient languages. They were written down after the Armenian alphabet was introduced by priests in 405 AD. Many of their ancient proverbs remain recognizable in modern sayings. Generations of families, including my own, continue to turn to cultural proverbs for succinct illustrations and thoughts. Thus, many have been included in the Destiny historical fiction trilogy. Here is an alphabetical collection of some Armenian proverbs and sayings, several of which appear in the three books and many more that do not. (For reference, I have tried to include the corresponding book and chapter numbers for those included in the trilogy.)

A calf is not found under an ox.
A drowning man will clutch at straws.
A friend is necessary in difficult days.   B 1, Ch 24
A girl with a golden cradle doesn't remain long in her father's house.
A guest belongs to God. B 3, Ch 11
A king must be worthy of a crown. B 3, Ch 30
A mountain won't get to a mountain, but a human will get to a human.
A mule can swim seven different strokes but the moment he sees the water he forgets them all.
A mule laden with gold is welcome at every castle.
A pain in the foot is soon forgotten. A pain in the head is not.
A woman is like the moon-some nights silver, others gold. B 2, Ch 32
Advice is a free gift that can become expensive for the one who gets it.
All riches come from the earth.
Always tell the truth in the form of a joke.

Ashamed of what she sees in the daytime, the sun sets with a blush. B 1, Ch 19
At death's door a man will beg for the fever. B 3, Ch 28
At home the dog is very brave.
Be learned but be taken for an ignorant. B 1, Ch 9 & 32
Before the fat one slims, the slim one will die.
Begin with small things, that you may achieve great. B 3, Ch 1
Better to be an ant's head than a lion's tail.
Better to lose one's eyes than one's calling.
Birds are caught with seed, men with money.
Bread and cheese; eat and dance. B 2, Ch 23
Chicks ought to be counted in the fall.
Choose a friend with the eyes of an old man, and a horse with the eyes of a young one.
Clouds that thunder do not always bring rain. B 1, Ch 24
Dine with a friend but do not do business with him.
Dogs that fight each other, will join forces against the wolf.
Don't be afraid of the turbulent river, be afraid of the moderate river.
Don't count the teeth of a gift horse.
Even a cooked hen would laugh.
Even if the nightingale is in a gold cage, she still dreams of returning to the forest. B 3, Ch 24
Far from the eye, far from the heart. B 3, Ch 7
First think, then speak.
Fortune visits only once. B 2, Ch28
Friendship is not born of words alone. B 3, Ch 27
From those who are given much, much is expected. B 1, Ch 3
Give a horse to the one who likes the truth so that on it he can escape.
God turns away his face from a shameless man.
He sleeps for himself and dreams for others.
He that asks knows one shame; he that doesn't knows two. B 3, Ch 22
He who cannot pray at home will celebrate mass somewhere else.

He who begs is shameless, but still more shameless is he who lends not to him.
He who falls into the water is not afraid of rain. B 1, Ch 22
He who looks for a friend without a fault will never find one.
He who sifts water does nothing useful.
He who speaks a lot learns little. B 3, Ch 2
He who steals an egg will steal a horse also.
He's looking for the donkey while sitting on it.
Honest men keep their promises. B 1, Ch 14
How can one start a fast with paklava in one's hand.
However much fruit a tree bears, it humbles its head that much more.
I do not advise the cat to strangle a lion. B 1, Ch 14
I know many songs, but I cannot sing.
If a brother was really good for anything, God would have one.
If a rich man dies, all the world is moved; if a poor man dies, nobody knows it.
If bread tastes good, it is all one to me whether an Armenian, a Jew, or a Turk bakes it.
If his ass wasn't attached, he would give that away too.
If not for your tongue, the crows would have gouged out your eyes.
If there was wisdom in beards, all goats would be prophets.
If you chase two rabbits [at the same time], you won't catch either of them.
In a town, if you observe that people wear the hat on one side, wear yours likewise. B 3, Ch 11
In business you need two Jews for one Greek, two Greeks for one Syrian and two Syrians for one Armenian.
In dreams the hungry see bread and the thirsty water.
Inside every man's heart is a lion that sleeps. B 1, Ch 14
Instead of opening your mouth, open your eyes. B 1, Ch 12
It is better to carry stones with a wise man than accept the meal of a madman.
Let me eat, let me sit, when it gets dark let me sleep. B 3, Ch 30
Love did not grow any garlic.

Make friends with a dog, but keep a stick in your hand.

Maybe he wanted to throw himself in the well, would you follow?

Measure seven times, cut once.

Men have three ears: one on the left of the head, one on the right of the head, and one in the heart.

Misfortune and fortune are brothers. B 1, Ch 29

No one is sure that his light will burn till morning. B 3, Ch 33

No other day can equal the one that is past.

Nobody casts stones at a fruitless tree. B 3, Ch 33

Not every piece of wood will become a ladle. B 2, Ch 16

Not everything round is an apple.

On a rainy day many offer to water the chickens.

Once we give shoulder to shoulder, we can turn mountains.

One bad deed begets another.   B 3, Ch 9

One blossom does not make a spring.

One can spoil the good name of a thousand. B 3, Ch 9

One idiot threw a stone in the well, forty wise people could not get it out.

One should not feel hurt at the kick of an ass. B 3, Ch 19

Priest on the outside; Satan on the inside. B 3, Ch 7

Rice is not cooked with only words.

She tells the sun: don't rise, I have come out.

Should the fear of the wolf make us forget our village? B 1, Ch 12

Silver money is to be kept for dark days. B1, Ch 28

Speech is silver; silence is gold.

Take up a stick, and the thieving dog understands.

Tears have meaning but only he who sheds them understands.

The blind have no higher wish than to have two eyes.

The bride doesn't know how to dance, so she says the floor is slanted.

The butterfly who settles on a branch is afraid that he will break it.

The calf that goes before the cow is devoured by the wolf.

The childless have one trouble, but those who have children have a thousand.
The eagle was killed by an arrow made from its own feathers.
The end of strife is repentance.
The feet of a lie are short. B 3, Ch 19
The gravity of the earth is so strong that the old grey man walks crooked.
The hound is lame until he sees the fox.
The kick of a quiet horse strikes strong. B 2, Ch 33
The meat is yours; the bones are mine.
The only sword that never rests is the tongue of a woman. B 3, Ch 9
The poor understand the troubles of the poor. B 2, Ch 31
The rose of wintertime is fire.
The scornful soon grow old.
The sun won't stay behind the cloud.
The tongue of the fool is always long.
The voice of the people is louder than the boom of a cannon. B 3, Author Ponderings
The water goes, the sand remains; The person dies, the memory remains. B 3, Ch 22
The water in which one drowns is always an ocean.
The water will find its way. B 2, Ch 35
The wolf changes its skin but not its nature. B 1, Ch 10
The wolf is upset about what he left behind, and the shepherd is upset about what he took away.
The woman who loves her husband corrects his faults; the man that loves his wife exaggerates them.
The world agrees in one word, time is golden. B 3, Ch 22
The world is a pair of stairs: some go up and others down. B2, Ch 28
The world is a pot, man but a spoon in it.
The wound of a dagger heals, but that of the tongue, never.
There is a life of iron and a life of silver. B 1, Ch 24
There is no reason for war that reasonable men cannot resolve. B 3, Author Ponderings

They asked a bullfrog, "Why do you croak all the time?" He replied, "I'm enchanted with my voice."
They cannot destroy Armenia. It lives on always. It lives within our souls. B 1, Ch 19
They make a camel out of a flea.
To ask a favor from a miser is like trying to make a hole in water.
To be willing is only half the job.
Unity is power.   B 3, Ch 10
Until you see trouble you will never know joy.
We cannot see with the eyes of others. B 2, Ch 24
What a man acquires in his youth serves as a crutch in his old age.
What does the blind man care if candles are dear?
What is play to the cat is death to the mouse.
What the great say, the humble hear.
What the wind brings it will take away again.
Whatever the eye sees, the heart won't forget. B 3, Ch 7
Whatever you sow, that's what you'll reap.
When a man sees that the water does not follow him, he follows the water.
When a tree falls there is plenty of kindling wood.
When asked, "What news from the sea?" The fish replied, "I have a lot to say, but my mouth is full of water."
When God gives, He gives with both hands. B3, Ch 20
When the axe came to the forest, the trees said: "The handle is one of us."
When the cart breaks down, advice abounds.
When the fox can't reach the grape, he says it's unripe.
When the thief has stolen from a thief, God laughs in heaven. B3 Ch 29
When they gave the donkey flowers to smell, he ate them.
When you are going in, consider first how you are coming out.
When you grow up you will forget it happened.
When your fortune improves, the columns of your house appear to be crooked.

Where is there a tree not shaken by the wind? B3, Ch 33

Wherever there's bread, stay there. B2, Ch 28

Wherever there's cheese, work there.

Whoever drinks on credit gets drunk more quickly.

Whoever works will eat.

With a soft tongue you can even pull a snake out of its nest.

You are as much of a person as the languages you know. B3, Ch 24

You cannot escape from destiny. B3, Back Cover

You cannot hit the point of a needle with a fist.

You cannot put a fire out with spit.

You don't satisfy your hunger by watching others work.

You never know a man until you have eaten a barrel of salt with him.

Quotes about Armenia

Proverbs, sayings, and expressions can give the impression that Armenian intelligence, understanding, and compassion were observed and valued by all peoples of the world. This is not true. Naturally, not all quotes and old proverbs are positive, nor supportive. Other cultures had their share of insults about Armenians. For example, consider the following.

"The salvation of the country requires the elimination of the Armenians."
-- Mehmet Talaat Pasha (1874 – 1921)
Ottoman Empire Minister of the Interior; principal architect of the Armenian Genocide

"Armenia was always a minority nation. The Armenians were annihilated by the Russians and then by the Turks."
-- Ernst Kaltenbrunner (1903 – 1946)
High-ranking Austrian SS official; Nazi Germany's Director of the Sicherheitsdienst

"Trust a snake before a Jew, a Jew before a Greek, but never trust an Armenian."
-- French saying

"One Jew can cheat ten Greeks; and one Armenian ten Greeks."
-- German saying

"It takes three Jews to cheat a Greek, three Greeks to cheat a Syrian, and three Syrians to cheat an Armenian."

-- Levantine saying

"If you can make a good bargain with an Armenian, you can make a good bargain with the devil."

-- Persian saying

"God made serpents and rabbits and Armenians."

-- Turkish saying

"In the 20th century, the Muslim world created a vision of religious nationalism. Turkey, for example, had to be ethnically Turkish. Kurds, Armenians, and other minorities didn't have a place in such a vision of a nation-state."

-- Feisal Abdul Rauf (1948 -)
Kuwaiti-born, Egyptian-American Sufi imam, author, & activist

"He was so depressed, he tried to commit suicide by inhaling next to an Armenian."

-- Woody Allen (1935 -)
American filmmaker

People who are Armenian or of Armenian descent are joined by students of history and the vast majority of world leaders in awareness and acknowledgement of the atrocities committed by the Ottomans. We recognize Armenia's thousands of years of heritage, including the population's fate as the conclusion of the Ottoman Empire approached. Generations of prominent people refer to the Armenians as they reflect on culture, history, and the need for humans to behave far better than we have in the past and continue to do in the present.

"Go ahead, destroy that race. Destroy Armenia. See if you can do it. Send them into the desert without bread or water. Burn their homes and churches. Then see if they will not laugh, sing, and pray again. For when two of them meet anywhere in the world, see if they will not create a New Armenia."
– William Saroyan (1908 – 1981)
Armenian-American novelist & Pulitzer Prize-winning playwright

"Let the Armenian people of Turkey who have suffered for the faith of Christ receive resurrection for a new free life."
-- Nicholas Romanov II (1868 – 1918)
Russian Tsar, 1894 – 1917

"The eyes of the Armenians speak long before the lips move and long after they cease to."
-- Arshile Gorky (1904 – 1948)
Armenian painter

"Our strength consists in our speed and in our brutality. Genghis Khan led millions of women and children to slaughter—with premeditation and a happy heart. History sees in him solely the founder of a state. It's a matter of indifference to me what a weak western European civilization will say about me. I have issued the command—and I'll have anybody who utters but one word of criticism executed by a firing squad—that our war aim does not consist in reaching certain lines, but in the physical destruction of the enemy. Accordingly, I have placed my death-head formation in readiness—with orders to them to send to death mercilessly and without compassion, men, women, and children of Polish derivation and language. We need not fear the judgement of history. Who, after all, speaks today of the annihilation of the Armenians?"
-- from German dictator Adolf Hitler's notes of his August 22, 1939, speech to his chief military officers one week before the invasion of Poland

"I am confident that the whole history of the human race contains no such horrible episode as this. The great massacres and persecutions of the past seem almost insignificant compared to the sufferings of the Armenian race in 1915."
-- Henry Morgenthau, Sr. (1856 – 1946)
German-born American lawyer & businessman;
Ambassador to Ottoman Empire during WWI

"Armenian is the language to speak with God."
-- Lord Byron (George Gordon Byron) (1788 – 1824)
English poet

"... the Armenian massacre was the greatest crime of the war, and the failure to act against Turkey is to condone it ... the failure to deal radically with the Turkish horror means that all talk of guaranteeing the future peace of the world is mischievous nonsense."
-- Theodore Roosevelt (1858 – 1919)
26th President of the United States

"The destruction of a civilized society by a jealous, violent one is never a good thing for anyone involved."
-- Marjorie Rowe Gulumian (1908 – 2001)
Author – "Of the Same Blood: Your Eurasian Heritage

"The year 1915 will be marked in the annals of civilization as the year of martyrdom for the Armenian race. No class of people has been spared – bishops, priests, ministers, and college professors were murdered ruthlessly."
-- Kevork Avedis Sarrafian (1889 – 1975)
Armenian writer; Bridgewater State University 1916
graduating classmate of Aram G. Gulumian

"I am Armenian, and I understand what it is to lose a country and lose a family and have massacres and genocides and everything against my people."
-- Andrea Martin (1947 -)
American actress and comedian

"We have all been hurt. We choose to either rush from our past or learn from our past."
--Jerry Tarkanian (1930 – 2015)
College basketball coach

"In 1911, Turkey established gun control. From 1915 to 1917, 1.5 million Armenians, unable to defend themselves, were exterminated."
-- Samuel "Joe the Plumber" Wurzelbacher (1973 -)
American activist

"Destroy all Armenians living in Turkey. Put an end to their existence, however criminal the measures taken may be, and no regard must be paid to either age or sex nor to conscientious scruples."
-- Talaat Pasha (1874 – 1921)
Ottoman Empire Minister of the Interior & convicted war criminal; in his September 16, 1916 directive to the government of Aleppo

"But history does matter. There is a line connecting the Armenians and the Jews and the Cambodians and the Bosnians and the Rwandans. There are obviously more, but, really, how much genocide can one sentence handle?"
-- Chris Bohjalian (1962 -)
American author

"You can talk about Holocaust denial, but it's really marginal for the most part. What is compelling about the Armenian genocide, is how it has been forgotten."
-- Atom Egoyan (1960 -)
Egyptian-born, Canadian filmmaker

"The legacy of the Armenian Genocide is woven into the fabric of America."
-- Adam Schiff (1960 -)
American lawyer and politician

"The few surviving Armenians no longer ask to go home. They do not ask for restitution. They ask simply to have the memory of their obliteration acknowledged. It is a moral obsession, the lonely legacy passed onto the third and fourth generation who no longer speak Armenian but who carry within them the seeds of resentment that will not be quashed."
-- Christopher Hedges (1956 -)
American journalist, commentator & minister

"On the eve of World War I, an estimated two million Armenians lived in the Ottoman Empire. Well over a million were deported and hundreds of thousands were simply killed."
-- Eliot Engel (1947 -)
American politician

"History has never been fair to the Armenians, and it is too late to start being so now."
-- Colin McEvedy (1930 – 2005)
British scholar, psychiatrist, & historian

"Speaker, with mixed emotions we mark the 50th anniversary of the Turkish genocide of the Armenian people. In taking notice of the shocking events in 1915, we observe this anniversary with sorrow in recalling the massacres of Armenians and with pride in saluting those brave patriots who survived to fight on the side of freedom during World War I."
-- Gerald R. Ford (1913 – 2002)
American military veteran & 38th President of the United States (from a 1965 Congressional speech)

"This was a tragic event in human history, but by paying tribute to the Armenian community we ensure the lessons of the Armenian genocide are properly understood and acknowledged."
-- Jerry Costello (1949 -)
American politician

"From May until October, the Ottoman Government pursued methodically a plan of extermination far more hellish than the worst possible massacre. Orders for the deportation of the entire Armenian population to Mesopotamia were dispatched to every province of Asia Minor. These orders were explicit and detailed. No Hamlet was too insignificant to be missed. The news was given by town criers that every Armenian was to be ready to leave at a certain hour for an unknown destination."
-- Herbert Adams Gibbons (1880 – 1934)
American journalist on international politics

"Concealing or denying evil is like allowing a wound to keep bleeding without bandaging it."
-- Pope Francis (Jorge Mario Bergoglio) (1936 -)
Argentine-born head of Catholic Church and sovereign of the Vatican City State

"In 1915 the Turkish government began and ruthlessly carried out the infamous general massacre and deportation of Armenians in Asia Minor. There is no reasonable doubt that this crime was planned and executed for political reasons."
-- Sir Winston Churchill (1874 – 1965)
British Prime Minister (1940 – 1945, 1951 – 1955)

"Moreover, as the leadership of the House confirmed last year, the Administration remains opposed to a congressional resolution on the Armenian Genocide due to Turkish objections. This approach sends absolutely the wrong signal to Turkey and to the rest of the world."
-- Patrick J. Kennedy (1967 -)
American politician

"I've had lots of discussions with my Muslim brothers and sisters who have said to me, "Christianity is a white man's religion" But I'm like, "how is that possible when Christianity went into Africa before it ever went into central Europe?" Even the first people to become a Christian nation were not Romans, they weren't the Byzantines either, they weren't the Greeks... the first people to claim a Christian empire were the Armenians."
-- Immortal Technique (stage name of Filipe Andres Coronel) (1978 -)
American rapper and activist

"Armenia remains a dream, a subject of stories; it is still, against all odds, a place."
-- Anthony Bourdain (1956 – 2018)
American celebrity chef & author

"Modern Armenia survived only because it was the single province controlled, and protected, by the Russian Empire. The rest of the territory within its historical borders is almost wholly devoid of ethnic Armenians."
-- John Shimkus (1958 -)
American military veteran, educator, and politician

"Armenia is dying, but it will survive. The little blood that it still has left is precious blood that will give birth to a heroic generation. A nation that does not want to die, does not die."
-- Anatole France (1844 – 1924)
French writer & Nobel Prize winner

"It is simply in the nature of Armenian to study, to learn, to question, to speculate, to discover, to invent, to revise, to restore, to preserve, to make, and to give."
-- William Saroyan (1908 – 1981)
Armenian-American novelist & Pulitzer Prize-winning playwright

"Almost unbelievable details of Turkish massacres of Armenians in Bitlis have reached Petrograd. In one village, 1,000 men, women, and children are reported to have locked in a wooden building and burned to death. In still another instance, it is asserted, several scores of men and women were tied together by chains and thrown into Lake Van."
-- from a news report out of London, published in the New York Times, August 20, 1915

"The association of Mount Ararat and Noah, the staunch Christians who were massacred periodically by the Mohammedan Turks, and the Sunday School collections over fifty years for alleviating their miseries-all cumulate to impress the name Armenia on the front of the American mind."
-- Herbert Hoover (1874 – 1964)
31st President of the United States

"The idea of telling the story of the Armenian genocide – or, really, any other genocide – and repeating those stories is really important."
-- Chris Cornell (1964 – 2017)
American singer-songwriter

"With faith and courage, generations of Armenians have overcome great suffering and proudly preserved their culture, traditions, and religion and have told the story of the genocide to an often indifferent world."
-- Jerry Costello (1943 -)
American politician & former U.S. Representative for Illinois

"Armenian folklore has it that three apples fell from Heaven: one for the teller of a story, one for the listener, and the third for the one who 'took it to heart.'"
-- Nancy Willard (1936 – 2017)
American writer

"The Christian Armenian story was the Polish Jewish story. The efforts of the Armenians to stay alive in Musa Dagh chimed with those struggling to survive the ghetto."
-- Howard Jacobson (1942 -)
British novelist & journalist

"Modern Armenia survived only because it was a single province controlled and protected by the Russian Empire."
-- John Shimkus (1958 -)
American politician & former U.S. Representative for Illinois, 20th, 19th, & 15th Districts

"Aid For Armenians Blocked by Turkey. Careful survey shows 55,000 persons killed in the vilayet of Van alone. The Turks do not deny the atrocities, but claim they are a military measure to protect them against a possible attack by a race that is disloyal."
-- published in the New York Times,
November 1, 1915

"When I was younger, I was listening to a lot of Armenian music, you know, revolutionary music about freedom and protest."
-- Serj Tankian (1967 -)
Armenian-American musician

"I was raised with a huge Armenian influence, always hearing stories of Armenia, celebrating Armenian holidays."
-- Kim Kardashian (1980 -)
Armenian-American media personality & businesswoman

"And I realized more and more that the Armenian story was not so much one of massacre and persecution, as survival."
-- Philip Marsden (1961 -)
English novelist & travel write

Armenian Contributions & Inventions

While we certainly cannot list all of the creative contributions made by Armenians, a few tidbits may prove enticing. For example, pop goddess **Cher (Cherilyn Sarkisian)** is an Armenian-American Grammy, Emmy, Golden Globe, and Academy Award-winning actress and singer.

Krekor Ohanian (1925 – 2017) is the Armenian-American actor (stage name: **Mike Connors**) best known for the TV series "Mannix" (1967 – 1975) on which he often spoke Armenian and quoted Armenian proverbs as Joe Mannix.

Ross Bagdasarian is the Armenian-American actor, musician, and film producer known by his Grammy Award-winning stage name **David Seville**, as the man who brought Alvin and the Chipmunks to life in 1958.

Flora Zabelle Maqangosarian Hitchcock was an Ottoman Empire born Broadway actress and one of the first stars of American silent films.

Easily the most prominent portrait photographer of all time was Armenian genocide survivor **Yousuf Karsh** (1908 – 2002). The Armenian-Canadian photographer held 15,312 sittings and processed more than 370,000 negatives. The Armenian Museum of America owns a large collection of some of his most famous portraits.

Arshile Gorky (1904 – 1948) was born **Vostanik Manoug** in the Ottoman Empire. The renowned painter is known as a leading abstract expressionism artist.

Many more Armenians play prominent roles in the ranks of artists, musicians, actors, dancers, and other celebrities from yesterday and today.

Many inventions also are credited to Armenians, both past and present. One of the earliest known credits comes from the oldest winery in the world, which has been discovered in a cave in Armenia. Interestingly, Greek philosophers, including Herodotus wrote about the delicious Armenian wines as early as the 5th Century BC. The following mark just a few more of the many inventions with which Armenians are directly credited.

Ottoman Empire-born **Luther George Simijian** (1905 – 1997) was a prolific inventor and an entrepreneur. Among other things, he invented the ATM (Automated Teller Machine) in 1939, the color x-ray, and the self-focusing camera.

Founder of the Delta Faucet Company and Masco Screw Company, **Alex Manoogian** (1901 – 1996) served as President of the Armenian General Benevolent Union (AGBU) and was awarded the Ellis Island Medal of Honor.

K. Cyrus Melikian (1920 – 2008) was an Armenian-American coffee industry pioneer, initiator of the Culinary Institute, and instrumental in numerous inventions including coffee pods and the in-machine coffee bean grinder. Co-founder of the Rudd-Melikian company, he earned the 1947 US Patent for the coffee vending machine.

One inventor has brought smiles to millions of faces with his waffle ice cream cone rolling machine. **Harry Tatosian** (1927 – 1989) received his patent in 1936.

Born in the Ottoman Empire, **Dr. Varaztad Kazanjian** (1879 – 1974) was an Armenian-American oral surgeon who became known as the founder of plastic surgery.

Though the first hair dryer was created by French stylist Alexander Godefroy in 1890, Armenian-American inventor **Gabriel Kazanjian** earned the first US Patent for a hand-held blow dryer in 1911.

Hovhannes Adamian (1879 – 1932) was a Soviet-Armenian engineer who earned a 1908 German patent for inventing the color television.

In 1854, Armenian chemist **Christopher Ter-Serobyan** from Istanbul developed the uncopiable green color for American money which is still used today.

Dr. Raymond Damadian (1936 - 2022) was the multi-award-winning Armenian American inventor of the **MRI** and the first doctor to perform a full-body scan of a person to diagnose cancer.

Michael Ter-Pogossian (1925 – 1996) was an Armenian American nuclear physicist and one of the founders of the **PET** scan technology. A nuclear medicine pioneer, he was a charter member of the American Nuclear Society.

Anna Kazanjian Longobardo (1928 – 2020) was the first woman to receive an engineering degree from Columbia University in 1949. She went on to make great contributions, especially in aerospace engineering and won the Egleston Medal for engineering achievements. She was also the first woman in the US to work on board navy submarines, destroyers, and other naval vessels. She also directed the development of radiation-tolerant computers for the US Air Force and served as the first woman executive of the Unisys Corporation's defense unit.

Armenian American businesswoman and entrepreneur **Carolyn Rafaelian** (1966 -) founded the "Alex and Ani"

jewelry company. She is listed in the Top 20 of Forbes'
America's Richest Self-made Women.

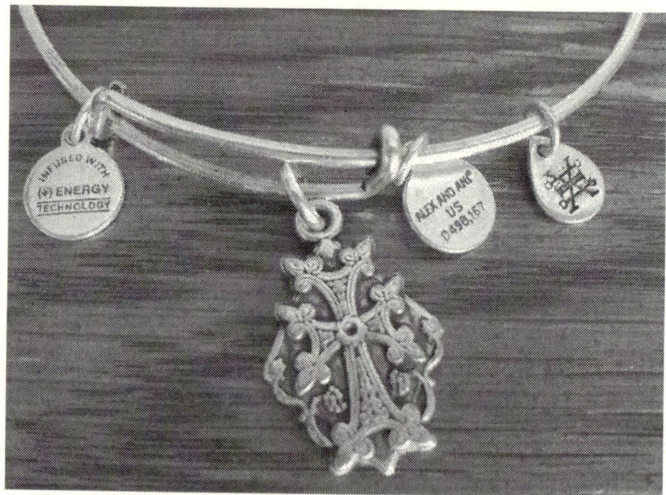

Author's Alex and Ani Armenian cross charm, a gift from
one of her mother's dear friends

Rose (Krikorian) and **Sarkis Colombosian** (1884 – 1966) are
credited with creating yogurt, which became world-renowned
through their Colombo label.

Born in Persia with a diagnosis of cerebral palsy, one
invention of Armenian-American **Emik Avagyar** (1924 –
2013) was the mechanism to convert a hand-controlled
wheelchair into an automatic chair.

The Quickie Wheelchair, the number one wheelchair used
by injured athletes was invented by Armenian American
Marilyn Hamilton (1949 -). A paralympic skier and
wheelchair tennis player, Hamilton used her hang-gliding
technology to develop a lighter, and easier to maneuver
wheelchair.

Ardashes Aykanian (1923 – 2016) invented corrugated straws for sipping beverages and was co-founder of the Flexible Plastic Straw Company. In 1968, he invented the spoon straw. Among his 40 US Patents is one for his Stay-bent flexible plastic straw. Other inventions included the sun strip for car front windows, plastic containers, and machinery for manufacturing plastic bottles of Coca-Cola.

The co-designer of the world-famous "MiG" aircraft was Soviet Armenian aircraft designer **Artem Mikoyan** (1905 – 1970).

Stephan Stepanian (1882 – 1964) was an Armenian American inventor and holder of numerous patents, including the elevator, the conveyor system, and the truck-mounted rotating concrete drum mixer.

The Armenian Zildjian family has been making cymbals since 1623. The family business, while initially based in Constantinople, fell to **Avedis Zildjian III** (1889 – 1979), who was born in Samatya, the Armenian area inside the city walls of Constantinople. Educated in France, he emigrated to America through Ellis Island in 1909 before founding in Massachusetts the first factory for the production of Zildjian cymbals in the US.

References, Resources & Further Reading

For online searches, please add a prefix http:// or https:// or simply www.

Armenian Cause Foundation ArmenianCause.net
Armenian Cultural and Educational Center ACEWatertown.org
Armenian Cultural Association of America ACAAInc.org
Armenian Cultural Foundation (Arlington, MA) no website
Armenian Embassy USA.MFA.am
Armenian General Benevolent Union AGBU.org
ArmenianGenocide.com
Armenian Heritage Foundation AmericanHeritagePark.org
ArmenianHouse.org
Armenian Institute.org.uk
Armenian International Women's Association AIWAInternational.org
Armenian Life Magazine ArmenianLife.com
Armenian Missionary Association of America AMAA.org
Armenian Museum of America ArmenianMuseum.org
Armenian National Committee of America ANCA.org
Armenian National Institute ArmenianGenocide.org
ArmenianReview.org
ArmenianWeekly.com
Britannica.com
Diaspora.gov.am

Ellis Island Foundation   StatueOfLiberty.org
EveryCulture.com
FacingHistory.org
ForeignPolicy.com
Genocide-Museum.am
Heritage.StatueOfLiberty.org
History.com
HistoryLearningSite.co.uk
Holocaust Museum Houston   HMH.org
LebaneseStudies.ncsu.edu
Military-history.fandom.com
National Association for Armenian Studies & Research
NAASR.org
NYTimes.com
OxfordReference.com
Reuters.com
Stanford.edu/Armenia

About the Author

Cathy Burnham Martin's first published work came in elementary school when an early poem won a town library contest. That was back when her parents refused to let her have the then-popular "Chatty Cathy" doll, stating that one chatty Cathy in the house was more than enough. Though poetry took a back seat, she has driven her writing and blabbing proficiencies along a highly eclectic career path through college recruitment, telecom marketing, corporate communications, TV broadcasting with an ABC affiliate, station management of an award-winning PEG-access station, bank organizing, and investor relations. An active board member and volunteer, she received Easter Seals' David P. Goodwin Lifetime Commitment Award. This professional voiceover artist, humorist, musical actress, journalist, and dedicated foodie earned numerous awards as a news anchor and businesswoman. She has produced and hosted groundbreaking documentaries, TV specials, and news reports, from the Moscow Superpower Summit and the opening of the Berlin Wall to coverage of Presidential Primaries. A born storyteller and business speaker, Cathy is a member of Actors Equity and writes daily articles for social media and the GoodLiving123.com website.

Other Titles
by Cathy Burnham Martin

(Destiny trilogy Books 1 & 2):
    Destiny of Dreams... Time Is Dear
    Destiny of Determination... Faith and Family
Good Living Skills: Learned from My Mother
Encouragement: How to Be and Find the Best
The Bimbo Has Brains... and Other Freaky Facts
The Bimbo Has MORE Brains...
    Surviving Political Correctness
A Dangerous Book for Dogs: Train Your Humans
Dog Days in the Life of the Miles-Mannered Man
Healthy Thinking Habits:
    Seven Attitude Skills Simplified
Of the Same Blood: Your Eurasian Heritage
Sage, Thyme & Other Life Seasonings: Perspectives
Fifty Years of Fabulous Family Favorites - Vols 1-3
Champagne! Facts, Fizz, Food & Fun
Dockside Dining:
    Vol 1 - Round One
    Vol 2 - A Second Helping
    Vol 3 - Back for Thirds
Cranberry Cooking
Lobacious Lobster - Decadently Super Simple Recipes
The Communication Coach:
    Business Communication Tips from the Pros

See all works from Cathy Burnham Martin
www.GoodLiving123.com

Partial List of Audiobooks
Narrated by Cathy Burnham Martin

Fiction

Destiny of Dreams... Time Is Dear
 (Violent content warning)
Destiny of Determination... Faith and Family
A Dangerous Book for Dogs –
 Train Your Humans with the Bandit Method
Kremlins Trilogy (Violent content warning)
 Citadels of Fire
 Bastions of Blood
 Dungeons of Destiny:
 An Epic Russian Historical Romance
Daniel's Fork: A Mystery Set in the
 Daniel's Fork Universe (Adult content warning)
The Relentless Brit

Non-Fiction

Encouragement: How to Be and Find the Best
Good Living Skills... Learned from My Mother
Healthy Thinking Habits:
 Seven Attitude Skills Simplified
The Bimbo Has Brains: And Other Freaky Facts
The Bimbo Has MORE Brains:
 Surviving Political Correctness
31 Days to a Stronger Marriage:
 A Guide to Building Closer Relationships
Exploring Past Lives: A Guide to the Soul's Travels
Why We Fail in Love: A Study into the Pursuit of
 One of Mankind's Most Precious Desires
The Hormone Fix:
 Naturally Rebalance Your System in 10 Weeks

Made in the USA
Columbia, SC
17 November 2023

25723920R00167